BEN AND I

OTHER BOOKS BY GENE BREWER

K-PAX
K-PAX II: On a Beam of Light
K-PAX III: The Worlds of Prot
K-PAX: the Trilogy, featuring Prot's Report
Creating K-PAX
"Alejandro," in *Twice Told*
Murder on Spruce Island
Wrongful Death

BEN AND I

A Christmas Story

BY

Gene Brewer

WITH ILLUSTRATIONS BY THE AUTHOR

COPYRIGHT © 2006 BY GENE BREWER.
LIBRARY OF CONGRESS CONTROL NUMBER: 2006909189
ISBN 10:   HARDCOVER   1-4257-1879-5
SOFTCOVER   1-4257-1880-9

ISBN 13:   HARDCOVER   978-1-4257-1879-4
SOFTCOVER   978-1-4257-1880-0

All rights reserved. No part of this book may be reproduced or transmitted in any form or by any means, electronic or mechanical, including photocopying, recording, or by any information storage and retrieval system, without permission in writing from the copyright owner.

This is a work of fiction. Names, characters, places and incidents either are the product of the author's imagination or are used fictitiously, and any resemblance to any actual persons, living or dead, events, or locales is entirely coincidental.

This book was printed in the United States of America.

To order additional copies of this book, contact:
Xlibris Corporation
1-888-795-4274
www.Xlibris.com
Orders@Xlibris.com

33665

to Juan Ramón and Platero
in the heaven of Moguer

CONTENTS

1: BEN	11
2: THE PARK	13
3: FRANKENSTEIN'S MONSTER	14
4: NATIONAL PASTIME	15
5: SIRENS	16
6: PIGEONS	17
7: CRAZY OTTO	18
8: ETERNITY	20
9: NEIGHBORS	21
10: LOST DOG	23
11: SNOW	24
12: APRIL FOOL	25
13: H'LESS BLIND VET W/ AIDS	27
14: SPRING	28
15: THE LAUNDROMAT	30
16: THE FLOWER	31
17: THE PIGEON MAN	32
18: HORSES	33
19: FRICKA	34
20: RAIN SHOWERS	35
21: LANDMARKS	36
22: CHURCH BELLS	37
23: THE VET	38
24: JOGGERS	41
25: THE RIVER	42
26: DREAMERS	43
27: BLOSSOMS	44
28: BEST FRIENDS	45
29: GRADUATION	46
30: REALITIES	47
31: THE PARADE	48
32: MIRRORS	50
33: THE MONGREL	51
34: BASKETBALL	52

35: THE STORM	53
36: THE BAT	54
37: THE SUN	55
38: PAVAROTTI	56
39: THE BANGER	57
40: THE WEDDING	58
41: CRI DE COEUR	59
42: NATIONAL HOLIDAY	60
43: DRINKING BUDDIES	61
44: STARS	62
45: NIGHT LIFE	63
46: TRASH 'N' TREASURE	65
47: THE MAGIC DWARF	66
48: SUMMER HEAT	67
49: OLYMPIC SKATERS	68
50: COURAGE	69
51: LIFE AND DEATH	70
52: REBIRTH	71
53: GULLS	72
54: THE BIBLE SALESMAN	73
55: TRUCK FARM	74
56: POTPOURRI	75
57: THE IDIOT	76
58: AMBROSIA	77
59: VINCENT	79
60: BRIGITTE	80
61: THE BLIND MAN	81
62: MUSIC	82
63: THE PRETZEL MAN	83
64: STATUES	84
65: GRASS	86
66: DEAD TREE	87
67: TWINS	87
68: STREET FAIR	88
69: THE JUGGLER	89
70: THE ELEPHANT MAN	91
71: LEADER OF THE PACK	92
72: BLUE SKY	93
73: PEACE	94
74: LEAVES	95
75: BOOKS	96
76: FILMMAKING	97

77: THE POET	98
78: THE CHILDREN	100
79: DUKE	101
80: HALLOWEEN	102
81: WINTER CHILL	104
82: BLACKIE	105
83: THE EXHIBITIONISTS	106
84: THE PREACHER	107
85: LATE AUTUMN	109
86: CHANGE	109
87: THE LAST ROBIN	110
88: REPAIRS	111
89: PERSPECTIVES	112
90: THANKSGIVING	114
91: FOG	115
92: CLEOPATRA	116
93: THE FIRE STATION	117
94: COLD WEATHER	119
95: GOODWILL	120
96: A NEW LIFE	121
97: HELL'S ANGELS	122
98: THE GOOD SAMARITAN	123
99: CHRISTMAS EVE	124
100: CHRISTMAS	126

1

BEN

I don't know how old Ben is, but when we go to the dog run in the park he is like a puppy. All the other dogs come at him, bouncing and yipping, while I fumble with his rope. They coax him to the center of the great arena, his ridiculous orange coat flashing from time to time like an enormous carrot among the blacks and browns of his entourage. They roll him over and the timeless Bacchanalia begins.

On the sidelines the spectators congregate to chat and watch the buffoonery. We never look at each other, and no one knows anyone else's name, only those of the dogs. "Ben is happiest dog in pahk," the Chinese woman tells me, and it is true, despite his cocked eyes and general clumsiness. But this has nothing to do with me.

It was nearly a month ago, on a cold February morning, that I found him pressed against the wrought-iron fence enclosing my living quarters, shivering and asleep. I opened the swinging gate—it is never locked, though I wire it shut to confuse would-be interlopers—and invited him in to share my breakfast. Without a moment's hesitation he bounded down the half-dozen steps and sat immediately with one cocked eye on my bananas, the other on the gate. One of his ears was bent back, giving him the absurd appearance of someone who doesn't know his socks don't match. Despite his enormous size and dearth of eye co-ordination he took the bites of fruit with the delicacy of a surgeon.

Everyone assumes we are homeless. That is not true. We have a home, we just don't pay rent. Although it suffers from a certain lack of amenities it is relatively warm in winter, cool in summer, and there is no doorman to tip. It is quiet and convenient to the park, churches, schools, shopping.

Camouflaged by a pair of large plastic trash cans, there is ample room for sleeping, dressing, and storage of all our belongings, which consist of an extra set of clothing for myself, a few cans of soup, a leaky air mattress, two blankets, a sketch pad, notebooks, a discarded thesaurus, and the usual odds and ends. In exchange for these facilities we keep an eye on the empty flat, beneath whose sidewalk we sleep, for the absent owner.

Ben breaks away from the group and runs over to me. I know what he wants. It's okay, Ben, I tell him, and he lopes to a corner for his morning bowel movement. While I look for a discarded newspaper to pick up the steaming excrement he bounds away to find his best friend, Fricka. But the nameless people are beginning to leash their companions and return to their warm apartments, the latter to doze and wait, doze and wait, the former to pursue whatever endeavors their lives have taken them to.

I, too, must work; I slip Ben's rope around his great round neck and we leave the park. He trots animatedly at my side as if we are going to the fair, though he knows full well it is only to the savings and loan, where I hold the door for people to come in and deposit their money or take out what they have put in earlier. All morning we work the door, Ben accepting the occasional pat of a familiar hand, and I the passing inquiry as to his health, though rarely does anyone ask after my own. "Have a nice day," I offer inanely to the tippers because they expect it, and to the penurious to shame them, though it rarely works.

By noon we are rich with nickels and dimes, enough for me to buy a day's meals from the Korean grocery and deli while Ben waits outside, his rope draped over the hydrant, never moving and never taking one or the other eye off the entrance until I emerge, greeting me as though I have just returned from a long and dangerous voyage.

It is an unusually clear day and we have lunch on the bench with the good view of the city skyline, Ben sitting attentively at my feet, waiting confidently for the last bite or two of my tomato and sprouts sandwiches, apple, and oatmeal raisin cookies. I give him a whole cookie. Ben loves oatmeal raisin.

2

THE PARK

If the shallow cave where we sleep is our bedroom, then the park is our kitchen, dining area, bath and parlor. Our favorite bench faces its entire length and we can see everything simultaneously: the chess tables, the dog run, the circular arena where the jugglers and musicians perform, the vendors. It is near the playground, and our afternoons are filled with the rich, innocent, untrammeled laughter of children.

From the north one enters the park through a huge concrete arch celebrating the inauguration of the father of our country. Statues of the Italian patriot Garibaldi and someone named Holley watch the passersby from their high pedestals, where they have stood for decades. But these are lifeless edifices which do not interest Ben and me, not when a microcosm of all humanity, its dogs and its horses, even the odd pet deer or parrot (an ostrich once) traverse the square day and night until they close the place at midnight to evacuate the bums and derelicts like ourselves.

It is surrounded by a great private university, whose main library and one of its attendant churches face us across the street from the southern boundary. Students of every discipline, yammering continually about the minutiae of their cloistered lives, frequent these hallowed sidewalks, oblivious to the plight of those who call the park their home: Crazy Otto, Mabel, Vincent the artist, the pigeon man, the Banger, and various transient drunks and other addicts, not to mention the squirrels, birds, rats, trees, shrubs and flowers which contribute substantially to the color and ambience.

But it is the sounds—the yelling, the crying, the barking, the laughter, the music—which continuously remind us that we are a part of nothing less than existence itself, with all its joys and sorrows. Life, whatever else it may be, is clamorous.

3

Frankenstein's Monster

Whenever we come across Mabel, the heavy-set woman who stays in the corner of the park, I always think of Debby Hatcher, the little girl at school who was so bundled up in winter that she walked like Frankenstein's monster: stiff-armed, stiff-legged, silent. She was such a prisoner of her heavy carapace that she could barely change course, and our teacher had to point her in the right direction and give her a little push toward home at the end of the day. One morning I came across her lying motionless in the snow, her arms lifted toward heaven in soundless supplication. It took two of us—myself and my friend Jack—to pull her up.

Debby's father was a minister, the hell and brimstone kind, who made her fall to her knees in prayer whenever she had done anything sinful, like dance spontaneously or talk to a boy. It was an effective system: she never spoke to me, nor to anyone.

When we got to the seventh grade and physical education became mandatory, the gym teacher was handed a note from Debby's father requesting that she be excused from the class for reasons of modesty. Unmoved, and perhaps suspicious, Mrs. Paxton made Debby play volleyball and take a shower with the rest of the girls. It was then that all the welts and abrasions were discovered on her thin little body.

But those were minor lesions compared to the contusions of her mind. When she was a junior in high school and unable to take another beating, and finding no surcease in prayer, Debby killed her father with a steak knife. She ended up in an institution for the criminally insane and I never heard from her again. Except once, I received an unsigned note with no return address: "Thank you for pulling me out of the snow."

Mabel hasn't tipped over yet, as far as I know, but she too can barely move in the three or four overcoats she always wears, those she can't cram into her mobile home, a huge canvas cart bearing the inscription PROPERTY OF U.S. POST OFFICE. Sometimes she naps on the bench she has claimed for her own, but when she is awake she is rarely silent: she sings or hums a medley of hymns, whose melancholy notes invariably wrench a sympathetic whine from my canine companion. She likes Ben but is suspicious of me, whom she calls "Po-lice." To Mabel, all white people are "Po-lice." Except, of course, for Crazy Otto.

I don't know what sort of Frankenstein created Mabel, or any of us, but for her and for Debby, the hell they were taught to fear at the end of their lives can't be much worse than the inferno they have already endured on this Earth.

4
National Pastime

So many things are happening at once in the park and on the streets that the vicissitudes of our little world fill all the streambeds of my consciousness. Yet, no matter how deep the rivers of recent experience, they drain away in the night and the darker memories of the past rush back in like the runoff from a sudden thunderstorm.

I saw a boy of five or six playing catch with his father today, though the temperature was in the thirties and every gentle toss must have seemed like a fastball to his untested hand. It is not this recollection, however, nor Ben's snoring, that keeps me awake this cold early morning, but the burning image of a snapshot of my little brother, who will be six in May.

The picture that floods my mind is of Chris in his Peewee League uniform. He is wearing his "Cubs" cap; a Louisville Slugger rests on his shoulder. Unbeknownst to him the bat has bent his left ear forward, like Ben's. He is smiling, but it is the fake smile reserved for the lenses of strangers.

It was almost a year ago that I took him out on a warm afternoon in mid-March and swatted grounders and flyballs to him for more than an hour. How my chest hurt that night! I feel the pain all over again as I recall that blissful occasion, but this ache is of a different kind and it won't go away.

Ben's ear comes up, an eye opens. He hears something beyond my ken. I wait: the sound of a horse clopping. It is quite unreal, as if we have been transported to a previous century. The clattering fades away, the pain seeps back in.

I roll over and thrust my cold hands under Ben's warm body. He rises stiffly, circles a few times and plops down again. Noticing, finally, that I am awake, he gazes at me and wonders whether morning is here. I tell him no, not yet. He is soon snoring again. I look up expecting to see the stars and, as always, find only blackness.

5
Sirens

Before Ben came I hardly noticed the desultory wail of sirens punctuating the narrative of the city, crying for lost souls everywhere. I had forgotten how acutely each frightened victim attends those harsh ripples of sound, to the exclusion of all others. Ben, who meddles in everyone else's affairs, hears them keenly. Whenever his floppy ears filter those awful ululations from the background noise (always before I do) he becomes profoundly agitated. Spinning like a dervish, his great mass picks up momentum as the blaring vehicle approaches. He whirls faster and faster, howling harmoniously, then gradually slows again as the cacophony finally loses itself in the general din. The spectacle never fails to produce smiles and laughter among the passersby, and even the odd dime or quarter from those who think it a staged performance.

His four-footed pirouettes remind me of the dances of bees, who convey life-saving information through such waltzes, and it is easy to imagine that Ben is trying to tell the police officer, the firefighter, or the paramedic where help is needed. They ignore him, of course, having no time for interesting phenomena of this, or any, kind.

The only alarms that leave him unmoved are the devices that are supposed to ward off car thieves. Even to Ben's sensitive auricles they are like the buzzing of flies: mere annoyances, whining irritants.

But his involvement with the ambulances and fire trucks of our lives is so intense, his keening so pathetic, that I wonder whether the sirens hold a special significance for him. Perhaps he was present at the death of his former guardian, or the fatal accident of a child. That might explain his unmistakable sympathy toward Mabel, as well as Crazy Otto, who roams the park bemoaning his lost son. And, for that matter, toward all of us.

Do you think there might be a world somewhere, Ben, whose inhabitants share your selfless empathy with their fellow creatures? A wonderful place where the deepest concerns aren't reserved for one's own difficulties, but for those of everyone? A utopia filled with dogs, where you would be king?

6
Pigeons

As Ben and I stroll the round sidewalk circumscribing the center of the park we are suddenly enveloped by low-flying pigeons. Instinctively I raise an arm for protection, but Ben merely tilts his head, and his nostrils flare and flare as they try to waft in the pungent essence of pigeonness. From all over the park they converge, aiming for the yellow bullseye of grain scattered by the man in the green flannel jacket. I can feel the wind of their wingbeats as the birds rush by, intent on a share of the free lunch. The cornucopia is already covered by burbling pigeons, hundreds of them. The stragglers land hopefully at the periphery.

We amble over for a closer look at the riot of chatter and movement. On my very first visit to the park I had marveled at the demonic red eyes and iridescent green necks with their double mauve bands, but I had not realized how distinctive each bird is. Reds and browns and whites and blacks mix and merge to produce a vast population of unique individuals.

Ben watches all the commotion with one eye while the other checks out an approaching Airedale for motive and intent. The pigeons, who were calm at Ben's slow, steady approach, babble a little louder, and those at the fringe of the feast waddle away from the intruder. The young terrier, in fact, breaks loose from his human companion and charges the assemblage, which takes to the air in absolute synchrony, the entire mass a single organism, and the park becomes a great merry-go-round of circling birds patiently waiting for the callow pup to sniff the abandoned grain and move on to other conquests. Ben glances at me and seems to shrug. Nearby, a child tries to keep up with his fleet-footed parents, noticing neither us nor the pigeons.

In another minute the picnickers are back as they were, an unorganized throng, each fending for himself. Ben's nostrils continue to take in every passing molecule of their gamy bouquet, seemingly unable to get enough of it. Long after the grain is gone, and only diehards remain, his interest has not waned; he keeps a sharp eye on the last of them as it takes off for one of the buildings surrounding the park.

Can you imagine a world without pigeons, Ben?

7
Crazy Otto

If I have a friend in the city, besides Ben, it is Crazy Otto. I do not call him this as a disparagement; that is what he calls himself. He likes the sound of it.

I don't know where Otto lives, but he seems to be well taken care of, at least in material terms. He obviously gets enough to eat, and his clothes are clean and mended. I envy him his warm bed, but not at any price.

He often shows up at the park without his pea coat, even on cold days like this one, but he is never without his navy blue knit hat. It's difficult to know how old Otto is, but probably older than his round baby face, pocked by some childhood disease, suggests.

Sometimes he seems perfectly rational, though he can break abruptly into hyena-like laughter. During these more lucid moments he is quite pleasant and informative, filling me in on the whereabouts and activities of the other park regulars, or discoursing on the failure of various governmental policies, his favorite topic. More often, however, he stands on the sidewalk across the street from the library shouting packets of knowledge to the students congregating there, ending, always, with "Richard! Be careful!"

It is possible that Otto was a member of the faculty at one time, which would account for his presence on the campus and his compulsion to lecture the undergraduates on whatever schizophrenic thoughts fill his head. He may have been an amateur athlete: he invariably interrupts his expositions to offer words of encouragement to the joggers trotting by, some of whom give him a thumbs up.

When his tortured mind is at peace with the world, as it is today, he hovers near the playground watching the children at their various forms of recreation—no speeches here. Not wanting to disturb these moments of tranquility Ben and I keep our distance, though we, too, enjoy the giggling and shouting.

There is one small boy who seems bent on flying a tiny kite, though his many efforts have failed to get it off the ground. Running hard, trying with all his might to get the lemon-yellow butterfly airborne, he crashes into the monkey pole, bloodying his nose and losing a tooth. Despite the noise and bluster he is ignored by his friends and scolded by his nanny, who then tries to comfort him and staunch the bleeding. But there is no one to console Crazy Otto, who is sobbing even louder than the boy.

It doesn't take much imagination to suppose that Richard was killed in some freak childhood accident. But watching Otto now as he vigorously applauds a student journeying peripatetically across the park on a unicycle, I wonder whether he isn't happier in his make-believe world, where his son is alive with laughter and a bright yellow kite sails high in the sky, than are the rest of us in our real world of greed, indifference and sorrow.

8
Eternity

After lunch Ben and I like to lie down on a sunny patch of grass, where Ben dozes while I survey the sky for signs of motion and change. Today it is full of those big, puffy, low-lying clouds which portend fine weather and good sailing. I start to point this out to Ben, but he has already fallen asleep, his broad, hairy chin stretched across my thigh. I wanted to tell him that when I was younger I used to watch such clouds, not because they looked like ghosts or dinosaurs, though they sometimes did, but because in those halcyon days I was filled with wonder about everything.

But I was especially fascinated by words—their meanings, their spellings, their beautiful, unique sounds—and I always thought I would become a poet, though no one supported such an idea. My teachers wanted me to apply myself to other pursuits, and my classmates all thought I was crazy. Even Allie sometimes asked me how I would support a family. Did you know I only missed graduation by a few weeks, my friend? I wonder where I would be now if I had stayed? And where *you* would be, too! Do you suppose that's what the scientists mean by multiple universes?

As if hearing these thoughts Ben opens one eye. Maybe that's what happens when we grow up, I suggest to him, we stop watching clouds. His good ear comes up and he gives me a look of patient understanding, though he, himself, will never grow up. He licks my hand even as the other eye ogles a pair of squirrels chasing each other down and around the oak trees.

Three resolute students rush by, lost in the intensity of their observations on sex and politics, as if no one had ever produced thoughts on these subjects as profound as their own. Ben sighs noisily before dozing off again. I pat him on the rump and gaze at a flock of gulls riding the updrafts between the buildings across the street, disappearing behind the water tanks and swooping up and around again, and again, and again. From the corner of the park: "Hot pretzels—softer than a baby's bottom!" Ben glances at me hopefully before drowsing off once more.

Above and beyond the intoxicated birds a jumbo jet climbs into one of the cottony clouds. I wait impatiently for it to break out and am not sure whether to be relieved or disappointed when it finally does. There is always hope for a kinder universe, where life is both beautiful and endless, and the gateway to this paradise may well lie at the center of a slow-moving cumulus . . . .

I don't know how long I have been contemplating the heavens but when I glance down at my companion he is awake and bathing his paws in sublime contentment. Ben, who doesn't know that he is going to die some day, has no use for eternity. As far as he, and the circling gulls, and the frenetic squirrels, and the happy, opinionated students are concerned, now is enough.

9

NEIGHBORS

When Ben and I leave for the park early on this cold, clear morning, our eyes are met by those of the skeletal woman across the street, who is returning from the corner market with a carton of cigarettes and a broom. My nod and hopeful smile are not requited; instead, she coughs drily and makes her emphysematic way up the few steps to her door. As always, when we run across one of our neighbors, I wonder whether this will be the last day in our subterranean haven, whether the old woman, or someone, will report our regular comings and goings to one or another authority.

But my anxiety is dissipated by the wonder of this crystalline hour, which is further intensified by the limpid chimes of the bell atop the Catholic school a few blocks away, the soft peal so intimate that it almost seems to come from within my own soul. Look, Ben, forsythia! See how it shines in the sun, like living gold!

My furry companion also seems jubilant, delivering a tremendous Eskimo kiss to a female Rottweiler, who seems as surprised as I. This *joie de vivre* continues at the dog run, Ben stealing and running with Luna's tennis ball, dropping it only to nab Fricka's rubber newspaper. The anonymous humans remark on the intensity of the sun, and all predict, predictably, a fine day. No one seems hurried or, if tardy, doesn't care. We linger too, and by the time we arrive at the savings and loan someone has usurped my position as unsalaried doorman. There is no point in arguing the matter, he is as needy as are we, and I have no claim on the spot.

Having nowhere else to go I sit down with Ben half a block away and absentmindedly set my cup down beside us. In my pocket there are only a few small coins, not enough for lunch, never mind dinner and snacks. I ponder our situation, grateful for the warm sun. Several passersby offer a gloved hand for Ben to sniff as they hurry along to important business engagements. A speeding bicycler, intent on delivery, nearly bowls over a pedestrian. "You dumb shit!" the latter yells. The cyclist doesn't look back. The man in the magazine kiosk looks at me and shrugs.

I give Ben a pat and suggest we try another location. But before I can get to my feet I hear the lovely, unmistakable tinkle of a coin falling into the cup. One of our regular customers, ignoring the petitions of the new door manager, has sought us out. Pretending not to notice me she gives Ben's ears a good scratching. No sooner has the young woman moved on than a quarter falls into the pot and, a few minutes later, a handful of nickles and pennies. At mid-morning the interloper skulks by mumbling, "Fuckin' goddamn cheap motherfuckers," and we return to our regular station.

Just before noon the mummy-skinned old dowager whom I call Cleopatra stomps into the building, summoning up an image of our elderly neighbor across the street. For some reason I can't shake the feeling that when we get home our air mattress and blankets and tiny cache of food will be gone and the gate tightly padlocked. Although I have learned not to worry about things over which I have no control, the absurd fear of homelessness gnaws at the back of my mind like Ben at a discarded soupbone. So it is with nervous impatience that we watch the pigeons and squirrels and humans pursue their sedulous afternoons and, finally, when it is dark, we hurry back to our own neighborhood to see whether we have been dispossessed, forgetting even to fill our water bottle at the stone drinking fountain.

But there is no eviction notice taped to the low brick wall, nor have our belongings been confiscated. Instead, someone has left a bag of nonperishable groceries inside the steel gate.

Ben immediately pokes his hairy snout into the depths of the heavy paper sack. I, equally spontaneously, croak a blubbery "Thank you!" into the silent, empty street.

10

LOST DOG

Under the arch a man stands on one foot, the other held behind him—a flamingo in faded jeans. Over and over he commands himself: "You won't remember; you won't remember; you won't remember . . . ." He is oblivious to Ben, who sniffs his supporting leg. In the center of the park a circle of students dance to an imaginary tune.

There is a sign posted on the great red oak tree near the run: LOST DOG. Below this terrible appeal is a photocopy of a mixed breed puppy lying on a large plaid cushion, a contented, doggy grin on his face. ANSWERS TO THE NAME SCRUFFY. A phone number is indicated.

All at once I am a boy again, following the well-worn path in the woods along the river, crying out the name of the only dog of my youth, a Scruffy-like stray who showed up one suppertime. My father, neither too sober nor too drunk, said he could stay with us, but he had to sleep outside. Mom gave him a bowl of leftover gravy and, for one wonderful year, there was always someone waiting for me at the end of the long driveway when I got off the school bus.

One afternoon he wasn't there. I could not accept the awful notion that he was dead, believing instead that he had ambled off in pursuit of far-ranging squirrels. Every evening for weeks I hung around the back yard with a bowl of gravy, hoping he would show up. To this day, nearly a decade later, I still entertain the possibility that he will come home, though there is no longer anyone for him to come home to.

Oh, Ben, what is more lamentable than a lost dog? Do you suppose Scruffy is frantically sniffing the sidewalks at this very moment for traces of familiarity? Or sick with fear in a nearby laboratory cage from which there is no escape? Would it help, do you suppose, to pray to the god of innocent children and animals to bring him back to his distraught companions?

A student wearing a BOYCOTT EVERYTHING T-shirt meanders by. At the end of her leash hobbles an ancient chow, nearly blind and probably deaf. When prolonged canine greetings have been exchanged and they have resumed their leisurely journey I hug Ben and assure him that if he ever got lost I would never, never stop looking for him. That if he should die I would bury him at the foot of the great red oak, where he would be close to all the frivolity and camaraderie. He licks my ear with such force that I topple over, and we roll in the grass like the pair of young lovers in running shoes frolicking behind that very tree.

The man under the arch incants, "You won't remember; you won't remember; you won't remember...."

11

Snow

We awaken to find our little cement entryway glittering with snow. I rise to an elbow and gaze at the lambent crystals, individually as unyielding as tiny diamonds, collectively more delicate than a termite's wing. Ben stands, stretches, and yawns noisily, like a furry piccolo. Suddenly he leaps over me and is up to his dewclaws in the sugary icing, his snout buried and snorting, a shaggy orange pig foraging for late winter truffles. Forgetting where he is, he lifts his leg and claims this frozen new world, already studded with pigeon tracks.

I find his bowl and clatter a handful of kibbles into it, adding a little extra to cover his energy needs for this crisp day. While he eats impatiently—always impatiently!—I munch on a stale pretzel, fold our blankets, and make a contribution to my own portable urinal, a plastic gallon jug. When we are both finished I lasso him with his rope and we set off toward the blinding eastern sun with a fresh excitement stirred by the sudden and dramatic change in the weather.

Ben is like a different dog. Everywhere we go he pokes his nose into the powdery snow, sniffing for buried treasure, rooting out mysteries. From time to time he rears his head, shakes it, and bares his teeth in a quake of silent laughter. His face is foam-white, as if he has been drinking from a bucket of beer. He lunges for every tree or post, marking each with a drop or two of his unique perfume. My hand hurts from the sharp tugs, the sudden changes of direction. I plead with him to slow down, but he ignores me as he does everyone who approaches, man or beast. He is fixated, a dog on a quest. This is not the aimless curiosity of the busybody; he is searching for something—a long-buried bone from an earlier snowfall or, more atavistically, a small hibernating animal.

As we jerk along it occurs to me that humans and dogs are alike in many ways, not the least of which is an abhorrence for having things secreted away, hidden from sight. For a brief, lovely moment I find myself feeling for packages in the coat closet, the alabaster dish on the shiny coffee table filled with candy and nuts, Mom stepping gingerly up the icy driveway hugging a handful of Christmas mail.

12

April Fool

March came in like a lamb this year and April, as unpredictable as life itself, also starts out gently. On this warm afternoon the park quickly fills with happy and optimistic people who sense that something sweet and good is about to happen. No one remembers, or wants to, that winter will come again as certainly as death.

Ben, too, discerns something wonderful in the air and, at the run, plays the fool, bowling over people and dogs alike, laughing insouciantly. The tomfoolery goes on for nearly an hour. I watch bemusedly as he upends terriers and collies and, finally, himself, roaring richly in exhausted mirth.

On our usual bench squirm a pair of lovers, shamelessly kissing and fondling with such passion that my own loins ache with desire for Allie. Ben grunts in disbelief when I tug on his rope and lead him elsewhere.

It has been five months since my father threw me out of the house and sent Chris to live with his grandmother, who can't stand me either. It's no wonder Allie wouldn't come with me, a high-school dropout, a would-be poet with no prospects. And who can blame her? I didn't want to leave, but I where could I stay? You understand, don't you, my friend?

A boy Chris's age skates by on new roller blades, a hint of a grin giving the lie to his practiced coolness, and he zigs and zags his way a little too fast through the strolling crowd until a cop, in mock anger, signals him to slow down. The boy, a little less cool, rolls along at a measured pace.

On the corner a heavyset man with a blotchy red face orders a pretzel for his granddaughter, who can't decide whether or not to take the proffered mustard. Grandpa shrugs his shoulders at the pretzel man and both, frozen in time like a life-size Norman Rockwell, wait patiently for the verdict. I want badly to suggest to her that she get a pretzel half with, half without, but, unlike Ben, I mind my own business.

Our second favorite bench is also occupied, this time by an elderly couple gazing lovingly into each other's rheumy eyes, as if for the first time. Ben runs right up to them, shamelessly soliciting a pat. An approaching siren precipitates a four-footed pirouette; the lovers laugh and applaud like children.

Out of nowhere comes a clown passing out colorful lollipops on looped sticks, his huge flappy ears triggering more smiles from the old folks. When Ben stops whirling, the clown offers him a red one. One of his eyes focuses intently on it, the other appeals to me for permission, which I cannot refuse. He takes the treat but instead of devouring it, as I expected, he tosses it high into the air, runs after it, tosses it again.

The kid on roller blades, now boasting nasty abrasions on both knees, skates painfully by. He has streaks under his eyes and it is all I can do not to reach out to embrace him and whisper something about life's endless setbacks and sorrows. But the clown beats me to it: his hand appears with a lemon-yellow confection dangling from it. The boy grabs the treat in triumph, as if it were the golden ring on the merry-go-round. His bloody knees seem forgotten as he glides away, his mouth bursting with color and flavor. Right behind him comes the little girl with her grandfather. She is chewing on a pretzel half covered with mustard, the other half plain, but she doesn't hesitate to accept a bright green sucker.

"How about you?" says the clown, and I turn to find an orange one free for the taking. My salivary glands respond instantly to the well-remembered tang. I take a good look at the painted-on smile, the uplifted eyebrows, the wiggling ears. But he is a phony fool, and Ben is only acting like one. The genuine article is sucking plaintively on a sunny orange lollipop.

13

H'LESS BLIND VET W/ AIDS

Sometimes, when Ben and I leave the Korean grocery, we pass by the man who sits beside a box, formerly a carton of French wine, supporting a hand-lettered sign announcing not only his impecuniousness but also his afflictions and military history. It reminds me somehow of a bumper sticker I once saw: NUKE A GAY WHALE FOR JESUS—it covers everything.

The man remains quite motionless, as he has for hours, perhaps, and the coins and bills pile up in his styrofoam cup. His clothes are ragged and dirty, his shoes worn through. As Ben takes a whiff at his kneeless trousers I peer into the dark glasses trying to get a look at his eyes, a glimpse of his soul. But they stare straight ahead and take no notice of me or even of Ben, who loudly and shamelessly snuffs at the man's unbathed crotch.

There was a time when my parents, in more prosperous days, took me to Washington to see the monuments, the government buildings, the tomb of the unknowns. I, like thousands of other youths, made funny faces at the guardians of the anonymous crypt, trying to get them to crack a smile. But, as far as those known soldiers were concerned, neither I nor anyone else was the slightest bit funny on that warm, cloudless,

June day. No one could penetrate those blank, shiny polaroids. I drop a dime into the styrofoam cup and, as we continue on our way, remark to Ben that perhaps all those guards at the tomb of the unknowns were as blind as he is, which would explain their extraordinary imperturbability.

A little later we come across another derelict who professes to be merely homeless with AIDS. He is at least as shabby as the other man, but his cup is nearly empty. Compared to the blind vet his plight seems almost inconsequential. I tell him about the guy a couple of blocks back who has already drained those who are inclined toward charity.

"Him?" the emaciated beggar snorts. He hawks and spits, and a shiny yellow blob joins a half-dozen of its shriveled brothers on the warm sidewalk. "That bastard ain't blind, he ain't a vet'ran, and he ain't got AIDS. Hell, he ain't even homeless! C'mere, boy." As he scratches Ben's head I feel a momentary wave of anger at the pseudounfortunate who seems to be making a bundle with his phony charade. But it is short-lived. How many of us, after all, are what we pretend to be? The man is probably just a struggling actor trying to eke out a living. But into my head pops an image of a retirement home for former guards at the tomb of the unknowns, the old codgers giggling at the slightest provocation, their long hours of unflappability behind them, free at last to break into a guffaw whenever they feel like it.

I, too, burst out in laughter, the reason for which I share with my fellow bum, and he laughs also, reciprocating with a joke about a panhandler who accepts VISA and MASTERCARD. Ben, wanting to join in the fun, throws himself on his back, inviting us to scratch his hairy belly. The three of us have found something wonderful about life: there is humor in even the most tragic situation.

14

SPRING

I awake to find Ben standing over me, whining. Before I can respond he backs off, dances a slow waltz to a faraway siren. When that urge has been satisfied he sits and stares at me, his head cocked right, then left, as I dribble into my plastic jug. While I am replacing the cap he picks up his rope in his strong jaws. It is the first balmy morning of the year—spring at last! I, too, feel happy on this day, and for good reason: the warmth triggers sweet memories of all the fresh, warm days of my youth, the excursions to the river and the ball diamond after long hiatuses. Older now, I am still eager to get out, but not before breakfast. We share a banana while I comb my hair and dig up a warm-weather shirt. Finally, and with a great clatter, we're off!

Ben sniffs the strong perfume of every crocus and daffodil we pass on the way to the park, laughs silently at the cooing, lovestruck pigeons who perform their ancient, shamelessly public mating rituals, responding to a force more powerful than all the atomic weapons in the world's arsenals.

But if spring is a harbinger of life it can also be a prelude to death. I shall never forget gazing out the window of my mother's hospital room at the budding trees and shrubs below, listening hard to the joyful songs of sparrows and robins, attempting to cling, for her sake, to the vestiges of life.

The fenced-in lawns of the fancy apartment buildings and the Episcopalian church are bright with grass, whose sheen is reflected in Ben's clear eyes. Poking his snout between the bars, he whimpers like a puppy. What a pity he can't romp on those verdant carpets, if only for one glorious moment. I imagine him loping happily around the periphery of those private compounds, sniffing every blade and playing tag with small, white butterflies. A yard like this always reminds me of my little brother (though he is more like a son!), who loves grass almost as much as Ben does. He used to tell me that it "itched" his feet and made them feel nice. I hope he still dislikes wearing shoes. You would love Chris, my furry friend—his heart is as gentle as a spring shower, like your own.

The park is not so grassy as the fenced-in lawns, but there are scattered patches and I turn Ben loose on one of them. He runs straight toward the homeless man sleeping on an army cot in the shady sector between the arch and the dog run, licks the stubbled face, and runs off. Startled, the man quickly raises himself to his elbows, but immediately flops down again to finish his beautiful dream. Ben, easily distracted, chases a black squirrel up a sycamore tree, for appearance's sake, then gallops back and we proceed to the arena. Inside, in his own joyful homage to spring, he runs and runs and runs.

15

The Laundromat

Having sold a subway token which Ben found in the park, and to celebrate the arrival of spring, we squander the windfall at the laundromat. I come already undressed except for my coat and shoes and a pair of topless pants legs, cut from someone's ragged discards, held up by strong rubber bands.

We arrive at dinnertime, when the place isn't so crowded—not to avoid waiting in line but to obviate the difficulty I encountered one late winter afternoon at a different establishment when I took off my clothes to put them into the washer. Although I kept my coat on while I undressed, one of the women present started screaming for a cop. None was around, fortunately, and one of the other patrons calmed her down before she could run out into the softly-falling snow.

Another reason for the relatively late hour is that a day's empty detergent boxes have accumulated in the trash container, providing enough residual powder for my wash. Within a couple of minutes both sets of clothes are swimming around in the hot, soapy water and I settle happily on the old wooden park bench the management has installed near the rinse tub, Ben at my feet. A young man, probably a student, also occupies the creaky bench. He is reading a book called THE RISE OF WESTERN CIVILIZATION. Two elderly women are busy at the folding tables and dryers. Once in a while they glance suspiciously toward us. I check to make sure all my buttons are secure.

A cockroach runs out from behind a washer. Ben raises an eyebrow. The insect, finding itself in the spotlight, hurries back to wherever it came from. It is then that I notice the cracked ceiling, the deteriorating walls, the rotting door and windowsills. Half the washers and dryers bear handwritten signs reading OUT OF ORDUR. I restrain myself from pointing out to my compatriot that civilization still has a ways to rise. It is not, after all, his doing.

The women leave and I seize the opportunity for a hasty sponge bath in the warm rinse water as it gurgles into the corner drain. The student gets up to take over their table space. "The dryer has a little time left if you want it," he offers, stuffing his clothes into a large black trash bag. As if on cue my washer stops spinning; I quickly retrieve everything and throw it into the unspent dryer. By the time I snap the door closed and return to the bench, the youth is already gone.

Except for the softly-humming machine, it is suddenly very quiet. Sweet-smelling. Warm. Peaceful. For a while, at least, we have the place all to ourselves, Ben and I and a family of cockroaches. And in that drowsy, fragrant, comfortable moment I wouldn't trade places with anyone else on the face of the Earth.

16

THE FLOWER

Look, Ben—look at the little daffodil growing out of the cement behind the wrought-iron fence! How strong it must be to survive there in the shadows, and how brave, living its life all alone, suffering its travail in silence. It reminds me of a tree I once saw growing from the side of the steep cliff at Cameron's gravel pit. Only after it had extended itself far enough out to reach the sunlight did it turn upward toward the sky. Have you noticed, Ben, that there are people and animals much like that intrepid little flower, that dauntless spruce? You have seen the man with no feet who lives on wine until they find him lying in a gutter and take him back to the hospital. And the skinny brown dog who sometimes comes to the park for scraps. The old pigeon, crippled and alone, who lost a wing some time ago, when it was run over by a motorcycle. And what about the rats and the cockroaches, whom everybody else is out to get? You know how hard life can be yourself, my friend, though only you know how long you wandered the streets before I found you huddled against that very fence where the daffodil now grows.

But did you know that the rest of the world is filled with creatures who manage to survive under even more terrible circumstances of poverty and disease and warfare, who live from hour to hour in hunger and fear, and never find a moment's happiness or peace? That, I think, is why this fragile daffodil moves me so much. See how it blows in the heavy wind? How it bends but does not break? You can be sure it will never give up its lonely struggle. Look closely, Ben, for on the face of that little flower is written the entire history of life on Earth.

17
THE PIGEON MAN

There is a man in the park who feeds the animals—peanuts for the squirrels, grain or seeds for the pigeons. We have often seen him pouring water from a plastic jug into shallow tin cans, the kind that cat food comes in, at the bases of the tall oak trees. He is the thinnest person I know of, and totally deaf. His green flannel coat is worn almost through.

Ben and I watch from a distance as he scatters something on the broad sidewalk for the pigeons, who come from all over the park. In the other direction Vincent, the one-armed painter, sets up his easel. A silver-haired man stumbles past us, followed at a distance by a younger one screaming, "Faggot! Go on, get out of here, you old queer!" Ben turns to look at me, half in fear, half in amusement. The feuding lovers, blinded by disappointment and rage, continue their sad, cacophonous march across the park.

Crazy Otto, on his way to watch Vincent work, stops to point out a faculty member who is never without his daily newspaper, though he can't read a word of it. The learned professor carries it only for show, Otto says, giggling like a child.

Out of nowhere a police vehicle—not a car, but one of those motorized golf carts—careens along the sidewalk toward the feeding pigeons. A blue light flashes but the birds don't seem to notice it, nor hear the whine of the approaching engine until it is almost upon them. Most take to the air simultaneously, as they always do when danger approaches, but three of the flock, slow to react for reasons of age or greed or inattentiveness, lie flopping amidst the uneaten food as the oblivious driver races on.

The old man rushes from one to the next, keening and pounding his head with his fists. One by one he gathers up the dying birds and gently deposits them into his grain sack. Two or three passersby turn briefly to see who is wailing; most hurry by without a glance. Clutching the bag, the pigeon man waddles down the walk on skinny, bowed legs; we can still hear his howling long after he is out of sight. The uninjured pigeons are already squabbling over the remaining grain. Vincent, the artist, violently slaps some paint onto his canvas. Otto studies the painting closely, doesn't seem to know whether to laugh or cry.

Ben licks my hand. He seems to understand something about what has happened. I, who understand nothing, pat him softly on the head.

18

Horses

Spring cleaning in the park, and an eager volunteer scurries over to request that we leave. Other diurnal visitors, similarly rousted, grudgingly gather their things for departure. On a nearby bench a sleeping drunk slowly rises, as if from the dead. "Daddy!" he yells. "Hey, Dad!" His head falls back with a bang, but he doesn't awaken, nor does he want to. The fresh-faced young girl bearing the eviction notice decides to let him lie. Mabel pushes her heavy cart past us toward the totem pole, in whose shadow she fruitlessly seeks refuge. Failing that, she takes to the streets, humming loudly.

Ben tugs me gently toward the police horses congregating at the corner, and we stroll over to say hello. The cops and I chat about the goings-on in the park and the health of its regular inhabitants; they seem genuinely concerned about the well-being of Otto, Mabel, the Banger, even ourselves. After that we watch their charges nuzzle my companion's snout as if he were a small, fuzzy horse and Ben, for his part, probably thinks they are very tall dogs. But the pretense doesn't work, for when he feigns a mortal challenge they stare at him in perplexity and high dignity—there are few clowns in their midst. Indeed, they always seem somewhat melancholy, as if they wished they were somewhere else, a grassy farm, perhaps, a flower-strewn meadow.

But these are beautiful mares, sound and well-groomed, and they invariably attract passersby, who can't resist patting the long, solid muzzle of such sizable creatures, whose magnificence, I believe, has something to do with size itself. Perhaps it is this same gentle nature in other large animals—whales, elephants, giraffes—that makes them so enchanting and distresses us so much when one of them falls or beaches himself.

I suppose that's one of the reasons Ben attracts children, who come at him from all directions hoping to commune with his great tolerance and compassion and, in so doing, to embrace all animals everywhere. Whenever a child hugs Ben my hopes for the future of mankind (and of the Earth) rise in proportion to the tightness of the squeeze, the sweep of Ben's wagging tail.

19

FRICKA

The sun dapples the wood chips in a playful manner, and the dog run is a chiaroscuro of light and shadow.

Everyone is here: Luna the pug, Daisy the greyhound, Pfeiffer the Pekingese—most of Ben's regular companions. Their guardians are relaxed and cheerful, as is their wont on warm and sunny Saturday mornings like this one, and the dogs know it. Even Duke, the German shepherd trained to attack anyone who touches his master, lopes around the enclosure less suspiciously than usual, growling at no one. Afflicted with spring fever myself, I am in no hurry to get to the S & L, though I had nothing for breakfast and need to earn at least enough money for lunch and dinner for the two of us.

Yet something is wrong with this otherwise perfect day, something phony about all the serenity and cheer, and I can't put my finger on it. As I watch the dogs bound after green and yellow tennis balls, the joy of life filling their canine souls to capacity, I feel a growing and profound sadness, which I can only attribute to a growing hunger. As always I long to see Allie, and Chris, too, but it goes beyond even that. After some moments of this puzzling disconsolation I remember that it was on a day like this that my mother died.

As I rerun that horrible event through the channels of my mind I am vaguely aware that Ben is loping toward me. However, he does not nuzzle my hand or lie down at my feet, as I expected, but at those of someone who must have joined me on the bench while I was preoccupied with life's burdens. I turn to find the Chinese woman, Fricka's companion, and a white plastic bag, the kind favored by shoppers because they are strong and easy to carry. Only then am I aware that I have seen neither her nor her Weimaraner for some time.

"Summer come early," she observes. Her free hand strokes Ben's head delicately.

"Yes," I answer inanely.

"Fricka—no more," she says, simply.

"I'm sorry." It all seems like some nightmare, and quite unreal, like the call from the hospital nearly two years ago.

"Fricka want Ben to have this." She reaches into the bag and offers me a chewed-up rubber newspaper. But before I can take it I hear the pathetic sound of whining. Ben, who understands everything, gently takes the toy from her tiny fingers, drops it to the ground, sniffs and licks it. The woman smiles bravely. Ben picks up the newspaper and drops it into her lap. Immediately she stands and throws it as far as she can, one last gesture, perhaps, to the memory of her dead dog. I watch as he gallops off to retrieve it. He hesitates only briefly (momentarily confused, perhaps, or held in the grip of memory) before snatching it up and fetching it back to her. But she is already gone.

She has forgotten her plastic bag. I stand up and search in every direction, but there is no sign of the aggrieved woman, whose name I never learned.

Ben and I peer into the bag. It is filled with cans of good dog food, with chewsticks and other treats. Ben whines again, but I cannot tell whether he is anticipating this windfall or mourning the loss of a good friend. I whine too, not only for recently-deceased canines and long-dead humans, but for all those they left behind.

20

Rain Showers

The rain pounding on our cement roof awakens Ben and me, but we lie still for a while because it sounds so pleasant and smells so good, like the showers of my childhood. It was in the big windowsill in the front room overlooking the lilacs and box elders and tulips populating the front lawn that I found a boyish kind of peace and security, where life seemed as if it would go on forever, even as my mother scanned the skies for signs of impending doom. If the rain came on a weekend I would spend the day watching my dad work at his bench in the garage. I still love the smell of sawdust, don't you, my friend? Did you know your own father? Did you like him?

The downpour slackens a bit but the wind picks up, and the route to the savings and loan is littered with flapping umbrellas, dying birds with broken wings. I inspect each reject as we slosh along, finally trade in "Old Yeller" for a fancy new black one, which is not damaged but merely inside out, a condition the previous owner was either too lazy or too rich to notice. Tacking into the gusts, we proceed to the workplace in comfort and style.

A man arrives at his parked car to find a window broken out, the front seat drenched. "Ah, *fuck*!" he screams. "They didn't even take the fucking radio! They're so fucking *stupid*!" Blinded by rage, he pounds the hood, kicks a tire. Ben offers unacknowledged condolences. Across the street a large black plastic bag rises from a grating and trudges off.

Outside the building a thriving business in cheap umbrellas has sprung up, as have identical operations all over town, no doubt. Don't you wonder, Ben, what these instant entrepreneurs do on cloudless days? Sell badly-needed tanning lotion, do you think?

The rain, like everything else, has its good side: no one resents our opening the door from the inside. In fact, the customers are more talkative than usual on wet days like this one. Inclement weather seems to equalize all of us, and the phony barriers of class and race come down for the duration. When it is pouring outside, there is an unmistakable bonding, as if against some sinister force. When the sun is shining, it's every man for himself.

21

Landmarks

As Ben and I traipse into the park for lunch on this bright May afternoon we encounter a group of Japanese tourists circumnavigating the square. I don't know how many of these well-dressed visitors speak English, but among themselves they do not. They are so engrossed in their conversations that some of them nearly fall over Ben and, after regaining their balance, apologize profusely to both of us.

Their guide informs them, through an interpreter, that the building across the street "may be one of the best examples of Greek revival architecture in the city." Several of the group dutifully snap a picture of it. As they move on, they resume their animated discussion, and I take a moment from my busy schedule to speculate on the nature of their conversation, guessing, finally, that it concerns the strange and unpalatable breakfast they were served a few hours earlier.

One or two stragglers, both men, turn to ask me, in palatable English, flavored by an unmistakable Swedish accent, whether they might take a photograph of us. I, holding Ben's rope in one hand and our lunch bag in the other, freeze for Japanese posterity. Ben sits, the cameras click, the two middle-aged visitors bow and hurry off to rejoin the group—off to see, perhaps, the houses of Mark Twain and Henry James.

Ben and I take our places on our usual bench. I open the bag; Ben thrusts his snout into it and whiffs loudly. The Japanese are still on the corner, still jabbering among themselves, and the cameras click and click.

What do you suppose their families and friends will think of all those pictures, Ben? And what will they say about the big orange dog and his hirsute companion when they appear unexpectedly in the midst of all the notable houses and beautiful buildings? Will we be famous all over Japan? Do you suppose they will laugh, or will they cry when they see us? It is probably true that we make a funny pair, my friend, and a sad one, too. But, of course, who doesn't?

22

CHURCH BELLS

Ben and I awaken to the sweet, gentle peal of the bells, which sound more like a flock of faraway sheep than a call to worship, on the little Armenian church around the corner. Although he has no more need of mankind's numerous deities than do I, we both feel a curious sense of tranquility upon hearing the soft, comforting, chimes.

I glance down at Ben and find him staring blankly at the trash cans, deep in thought, his massive head resting lightly on my knee. I reach forward and scratch an ear. One of his eyes rolls toward me, his tail thumps twice, and we return to our respective reveries.

Before my dad became a practicing alcoholic, the best time of the week was Sunday morning. It began with a leisurely and substantial (invariably pancakes and sausages) breakfast in the sunny kitchen, a close scrutiny of the comics, maybe a quick stamp inventory or a small job on the Erector set. Radio and TV were prohibited that morning. The peace and beauty of the hour was overwhelming. And then came the sound of church bells and the smell of dinner already in the oven . . . .

The trot and snorting of a jogger come into range, heavy feet pound across our roof. My concentration is broken, and so is Ben's; I notice for the first time the musty smell of our subterranean apartment, still damp after yesterday's hard rain. When the noise has abated he turns his head toward me and commences his famous one-eyed stare, which will not terminate until I show some sign of activity. I return his steady gaze for a few seconds but, as always, I lose the contest with an unpreventable laugh. His tail moves in earnest now, but the awful glare will continue until I get up and produce some victuals. It's time, anyway, to head for the church on the square and our duties there as God's doormen.

But just as I am about to take action the bells toll again, and once more Ben becomes dreamy, his hunger stayed for a moment by the beauty of the dulcet notes and, perhaps like me, by memories of happy bygone days: a warm stove, a church organ, an early Sunday dinner.

23

The Vet

On the way to the park Ben stops suddenly and does his business on the sidewalk, which is unusual for him. A student toting a huge portfolio of sketches and wearing the striped leotards popularized by Mammy Yokum passes by, pretending not to notice us. Despite the bulky load, she skips every third step.

When I bend over to pick up Ben's excrement I notice blood in it. I am alarmed: did he get into the rat poison yesterday when he darted off to chase the black squirrels? Clutching his bloody stool in a discarded newspaper I straighten up to see the girl in the striped leotards looking back at us as she skips around the corner.

Ben doesn't act sick and, after generously watering a tree, takes up the trail of some animal who may have passed by a week earlier. Nevertheless, I turn him around and lead him back the way we came, toward the animal hospital. Delighted with this unexpected break in the usual routine he bounds ahead of me with enthusiasm. I take my eyes off him only long enough to study the upcoming traffic lights. In the middle of the street he stops to defecate again, but nothing appears except for some bloody slime. A taxi stops to let him finish. The driver shrugs.

We are forty-five minutes too early. I peer between the slats in the blinds, but find no sign of life. Ben, having sniffed at the door, knows exactly where we are and wants to leave. Trying to calm his anxiety I sit down beside him on the curb. He paces back and forth behind me for a while then lies down on the sidewalk, one eye on me and the other on the veterinarian's door. Two or three passersby, proffering a hand for Ben to sniff, inform me that the hospital doesn't open for half an hour. Ben's tail wags only feebly, not because he is ill but because he wants to be somewhere else. Both his ears are in constant motion, a pair of fuzzy radar dishes searching for signs of pain and distress. He gets up, lies down, gets up again.

A light comes on! I tap on the dirty window. There is no response. I knock louder. A young woman impatiently spreads the blinds. "Emergency!" I shout. Her scowling face disappears and two disembodied hands poke through the slats, one pointing to the wristwatch on the other. I pound and shout louder, "Emergency!

Emergency!" There is no response. I peer through a crack: she is sitting on the counter filing her nails.

Fifteen minutes later the shades open. She points matter-of-factly to the door. I coax Ben over to it, but it won't open. I press the button on the intercom. "Yes?" a voice inquires.

"It's us, goddammit!" I shriek. There is a buzz and we are allowed admittance. Ben tries to go the other way.

"May I help you?" the girl inquires indifferently.

I pretend to regain my composure. "I didn't mean to yell," I apologize. "My dog is very sick. Could we see the vet?"

"Do you have an appointment?"

"It just happened. He's bleeding from the rear end."

She takes a sip of coffee, flips to her day's schedule. "How about 5:15?" she suggests. Her features are sharp—nose, chin, ears—all pointed.

"He's very sick," I plead. "Can't you get us in sooner?"

By now she has noticed that my clothes are tattered and unpressed. "How did you plan to pay?" she demands as she picks up the nail file.

The vet appears. He is huge, at least six feet six, and gorilla stocky. Snarling something about an unfilled order, he pokes into his ear with a little finger. He appears not to notice me; his gaze focuses on Ben, who wags his tail hopefully. "Bring him in," he commands. His voice echoes around and around the empty waiting area. Ben's tail stops wagging.

It's only a bacterial infection, for which Ben receives a vial of tiny white pills. He also gets all the necessary shots, a rabies certificate, and a license tag, which the vet clamps onto his rope with a pair of pliers. The cocked eyes and bent ear, however, can't be fixed. Despite the needles and the thermometer and the sour demeanor, Ben licks him in the face.

"How much do I owe you?"

Gruffly: "Nothing. Ben just paid me."

"At least let me clean your windows."

"Not necessary. But if you want to, I'll get you a bucket." He seems annoyed.

For the rest of the morning I wash the windows, inside and out, the sills, the blinds, the radiators. Ben greets all the dogs and cats as they come in, assures them that it won't be as bad as they think. The receptionist scowls at us whenever she turns our way. But Ben and I are on to her, and we return huge grins.

24

JOGGERS

The sidewalk around the park is decorated by a rainbow of joggers running for their lives. Some, no doubt, have been at it for years, though most, like the squirrels, have spent the harshest winter months in comfortable hibernation. Ben and I watch with amusement the bounding parade of the porcine and unfit.

Except for one nonagenarian with a long drool hanging from his stubbly chin, the males, for the most part, are indistinguishable: middle-aged, serious, they grimly pound out their self-imposed quotas. The women are a different matter entirely. A spectrum of style, both running and attire, most plod wearily around the square toward the corner they started from, hoping, if not to turn back the clock, to stop its ticking for a little while. Few of the runners are students, who have not yet learned they are mortal and, in any case, have no time for such concerns.

One of the fair-weather zealots, a forty-fivish woman with large hips and bouncing breasts, captures our attention. She slaps along, eyes downward, lost in the roar of her appended Walkman. Again and again she circles the park, seeing nothing but her own swollen Nikes, hearing nothing but the music pounding inside her head. Across from the library Otto cheers her on. She pushes agonizingly forward, foot after foot, as dozens of other runners pass her by, even the slavering geezer. Our amusement turns to melancholy as we watch, and then somehow become part of, her losing battle.

As she begins the fifth lap of her long, if not lonely, journey, her pained expression abruptly changes to one of surprise and puzzlement, followed immediately by something like exaltation. Her body, like that of a headless chicken, plods on for a few more steps before it understands what her brain is telling it and comes to a complete halt. She pulls the earphones and radio from her matted hair and soaked sweatshirt and flings them toward a trash container.

Heading for the corner and home she notices, for the first time, that we are watching her. She lets out a little blurt, halfway between a laugh and a sob, which we return. The other joggers struggle on and on, unaware that one of them has truly and finally cheated death.

25

THE RIVER

Whenever I feel the claws of depression clutching at my heart I head for the river, whose primitive scent takes me back immediately to the happy optimism of my childhood, when the most important thing in the world was to skip a flat rock perfectly (though I never quite succeeded) over the surface of the slow-moving stream that ran through the nearby woods. How I long for those years of simplicity and innocence! I hope Chris has found a pond or river near Grandma's farm to skip rocks on warm summer mornings.

A block from our destination a worn old man bearing two huge bags of empty cans and bottles on his back, and looking very much like a giant insect, shuffles by on his way to the recycling machine at the nearest market. His pants, several sizes too big, sag at the waist. Though bent by his hard-won burden, he is smiling. Ben sniffs at his drooping cuffs.

A group of barely adolescent boys wearing baseball uniforms have also come to the river to practice on its concrete banks, though they do more yelling than throwing or fielding. How I would love to join them, to feel the solid comfort of a baseball in my hand, to swing a bat once more. Would they let us play, do you suppose, my friend?

Few other people are around, and I let Ben run free. Farther upriver, where the barges used to dock, two brothers of about eight and ten dart past and run out onto the smaller of the two crumbling piers. Ben, who loves to chase anything on the move, bounds after them. Afraid that he might scare them, or attempt to bowl them over, I run shouting after him. But the boys spot him and, like most children, turn to receive him, dropping simultaneously to their knees for big hugs and sloppy kisses. Then they proceed to the end of the pier, Ben loping ahead to sniff out its recent history. Finally, loaded with information, he trots contentedly back to me.

Look Ben, they're skipping rocks (or the cement chips that pass for rocks in the city)! My depression gives way to a growing happiness. Though I wish with all my might that those two boys could be Chris and myself, I am buoyed by the knowledge that innocence, if seriously ill, is still alive on the banks of broad rivers and narrow streams everywhere.

C'mon, Ben, let's see if I can't make just one perfect throw!

26
Dreamers

What a wonderful dream I had, Ben! Do you suppose it had anything to do with the warm sunshine on our faces? You look quite content—did you have a nice nap too, my friend?

Shall I tell you about mine? You were in it. We were walking along the edge of a forest—you, Allie, Chris and I, and my mother and father. The sun was very bright, as though its light were unfiltered or magnified, and the sky a rich, deep blue. The trees were alive with birds, like the new little elm trees over by the movie theater—teeming with vitality, color, and song. In the open fields to our left all the animals in the zoo roamed free: elephants, giraffes, wolves, bears. Ahead I could see a beach. The ocean was a beautiful aquamarine, filled with whales and porpoises and, I suppose, all the incredible varieties of fish and other creatures of the sea. The air itself smelled as sweet as honeysuckle.

We strolled along in absolute contentment, Allie and I making plans for the future, Chris chasing after you and vice versa. But before we got to the coast we came to a little park filled with dogs and horses, all running unfettered and free. How you loved the tall grass! I can still see you galloping through it, eyes straight, ears unbent.

And guess who else was there? Otto! Not the crazy man in the navy blue knit hat, but the real professor conversing happily with his son, Richard, holding his hand tightly so that he wouldn't run into any danger. And Mabel, wearing only one overcoat, arm in arm with a handsome, gray-haired man about her age, and jabbering, as always, but with intelligence and humor. Birds were everywhere, feasting on piles of grain and bread crumbs scattered by the pigeon man and his disciples at every corner.

Where do you suppose unlived dreams go, Ben, unspoken thoughts? Straight to heaven, like golden wraiths? Not quite—they tarry awhile before leaving us. Even though I am awake now and back to sad reality, it seems that the whole world is filled, at this moment, with love and happiness and beauty.

27

Blossoms

Ben, who spends more time at play than most children, loves to roll in the cherry blossoms, which fall steadily, silently in the warm afternoon breeze, like pink summer snow. He twists and snorts, whirls and grunts, chases his upside-down tail. When he finally arises from the sweet-smelling earth he shakes himself end to end and the blossoms fly away before drifting slowly, softly to the ground. Some of them stick to his shaggy coat, and he trots to the dog run adorned with precious jewels.

Halfway there we come across a trio of little girls in fluffy dresses and shiny black shoes. Each holds a small, bright package to her breast and a matching smile on her well-scrubbed face. Forgetting their happy mission they surround Ben at once, squealing and stroking his moplike coat, in which several pink blossoms are still matted. One of them tries to climb onto his back. I glance at their chaperone, an older sister, perhaps, who has long wanted "a big dog like that," and she allows me to lift the weightless bodies, one at a time, onto his shoulders for a short prance. When the rides are over, Ben, ever the clown, grabs one of the presents in his jaws and pretends to run off with it. The girls squeal and squeal as he drops it, as gently as if it were a robin's egg, at the base of a nearby sycamore. A creature of short concentration span himself, he lopes off immediately in fruitless pursuit of a black squirrel.

The older girl brushes some dog hair from the blue, pink and yellow dresses and they all skip away on the warm breeze. Ben, returning from the chase, gazes wistfully after them, perhaps realizing that I am thinking about Allie's sixteenth birthday party. I tell him that blossoms are ephemeral treasures and soon lost, but that with their passing will come other flowers, other petals. He seems as little consoled by this empty wisdom as am I.

28
Best Friends

Since the demise of Fricka, Ben has tried hard to befriend Daisy, the neurotic greyhound, whose guardian is as mystified as anyone about her fear of humans and dogs alike. The effort has paid off: whenever we come to the dog run Daisy is often waiting at the gate for Ben to show up. Together they bound away to join the others and, no matter what happens, she never strays far from his calming presence. He is her mentor, her protector, her best canine friend. When her human companion, a young man whose head is egg bald, leashes her for the trip home, she is heartbroken. "If you ever want to sell Ben—" he begins, ending abruptly at my incredulous stare. As they leave the run Daisy glances sadly in our direction.

The park is rich with people today—individuals, couples, groups of three or four—the numbers swollen by students and faculty who have completed their final exams and are awaiting graduation. There is an air of melancholy, a realization that something is ending, and it is forever. Thoughts are conveyed less by words than by touches and expressions. Even the drug sellers appear reserved, pensive.

Two attractive young women wearing shorts and see-through T-shirts proclaiming lesbian rights stroll hand in hand along the diagonal sidewalk, oblivious to the stares of the righteous, or anything else, their eyes locked onto each other's souls. I envy them their moment of unabashed bliss.

A mixed race-nationality-gender couple come by in the other direction. The man offers a hand, palm-up, to Ben, who licks it and wags his tail. His friend beams, says something in one of the world's countless languages, and laughs. Her teeth are the whitest I have ever seen, even whiter than Allie's. The man utters a polite "T'ank you" (to Ben, not to me) and the happy pair drifts away, the woman still giggling.

An older couple, both male, cross their path. They neither converse nor hold hands, but they exude the contentment of those who have shared a long and happy relationship, though their eyes contain more than their share of sadness as well. A boy runs up, hugs Ben, is resorbed by the crowd.

We watch the parade all afternoon, Ben scoring on hug after hug, until I can no longer resist hugging him myself. Surprised, he rolls over onto his back and one eye gazes deeply into mine. I rub his inviting belly, and in my pocket I find a cookie I have stashed away for just such a moment.

29

GRADUATION

When Ben and I visit the dog run this early morning we find several identical gray-clad workers setting up bleachers in the middle of the park. They work wordlessly, efficiently. Bang, bang, bang, bang, and another one is ready. A nondescript truck creeps along the sidewalk, stops with a mousy squeal. Two men climb out and a herd of dusty blue barricades is unloaded. The sun, already bright in the sky, electrifies everything it touches, elevating these quotidian pursuits to affairs of intensity and significance. Even the savings and loan seems magnificent today, and our cup fills quickly.

On our way back to the park for our picnic lunch we hear the loudspeakers blaring enthusiasm for human ingenuity and free enterprise. The speech is interrupted several times by the applause of the ecstatic crowd, who would cheer Ebeneezer Scrooge on this happy occasion. I recall Allie's brother's graduation, with its glorious sense of accomplishment and promise, his eagerness to "change the world." Then everything comes back with a rush: a yellow school bus, a warm day, a proud report card, cries of "School's out, school's out, teacher let the monkeys out!"

In a corner of the park, where all the uninvited are sequestered, Ben and I find a sunny patch of unoccupied dirt with a tree to lean against. His unmatched ears, scanning the noise and folderoll for important events, rotate constantly. I munch my cucumber sandwich and listen as someone promises a glorious future for everyone everywhere, filled with opportunity and reward. "Oh, there are problems to be solved," the speaker shrieks, "but together we can do anything we set our minds to." The audience cheers wildly. At the top of the arch a young man clutching a trumpet peers down at the crowd. I experience a wave of vertigo for his sake, and try to will him to step back from the edge. A girl in a purple robe rushes by holding down her mortar board with both hands.

A bass replaces the shrieking soprano, but the message is the same: "This is the best possible moment to be graduating from a great university in the history of mankind," he begins quietly, almost in a whisper, then waits for the cheers to reach such a crescendo that Ben looks at me with one eye while the other studies the roaring bleachers for signs of trouble. I pat his flank, reassuring myself as much as him. The young man above us has set down his trumpet and is leaning far out over the top of the arch with a camera, trying to focus on the people meandering directly below him. I hold my breath. At last he snaps his picture and retreats from the precipice. Gratefully I resume eating.

The speeches are finally over and the deans come forward to anoint their protégés, each molded in his or her own image, none of whom would be recognized by their august mentors if encountered on the street. Those upon whom these official kudos are bestowed cheer themselves one final time, and an army of purple bodies erupts onto the sidewalks, eager to go out and change the world.

School's out, school's out, teacher let the monkeys out!

30

REALITIES

Crazy Otto approaches Ben and me with that unmistakable air of distracted determination characteristic of faculty members on their way from classroom to committee meeting and back again, and I understand at once that he is reliving a day in the distant past, a happier time he visits now and then.

After giving Ben his customary ear scratch and tummy rub Professor Otto joins me on the bench. He enjoys talking with me, I believe, because I pretend to follow the thread of his discourse, a mixture of history and philosophy, delivered in the strong, confident tones of the lecturer. He is particularly interested in whatever realities might lie outside our own. Where, perhaps, Richard has gone, and where they will meet again some day. The irony of this, in view of his regular passage into his own private world, does not escape my attention.

Someone with unruly green hair, like the top of a pineapple, strolls by, engaged in intense conversation with himself. Farther down the sidewalk stands an old man wearing a thin brown overcoat, and whose feet are wrapped in rags. It strikes me that he is waiting there to die. All at once he comes to life: he paces briskly for half a minute, stops, whirls around and returns to his starting place near the body of a dead squirrel. It occurs to me that perhaps the man was once a sentry at the tomb of the unknowns.

Before he goes, Otto mentions that he is keeping Mabel's post office cart safe for her—she is in the hospital again, suffering from dehydration and high blood pressure. She won't drink because she doesn't like to go into the public restroom to urinate, and she won't take her pills because someone is trying to poison her. Her proof of this is that the pigeons won't touch them. Otto laughs explosively and, just as abruptly, stops. He rises and tells me he has to get to the library to prepare for tomorrow's lecture. One last pat and he is off, whistling a tune of his own creation.

Ben bathes his paws with the contentment of a dog who knows it is not long until suppertime.

31

The Parade

On almost any given day there is a parade somewhere in the city and, when one comes by the park, Ben wants a front row seat, where he won't miss anything. I, on the other hand, like to watch the eager faces of the children on the sidelines.

The mayor, on foot, leads things off, and all the kids stare in awe, though they don't know what a "mayor" is, only that their parents are pointing him out with excitement in their voices. A surprisingly small man, he flashes Ben and me a genuinely warm, even childlike, smile. He has our vote, Ben!

His honor is followed by scores of police officers, who also beam, though less professionally, and wave self-consciously to the crowd. Though none of the children knows any of the cops personally, television has succeeded in creating a sense of respectful familiarity toward them. I remember asking Chris once what he wanted to be when he grew up. His first choice was "Captain Kirk!" The next was "A policeman, I guess."

The officers are followed by clowns on unicycles, who pass out balloons to excited pre-schoolers, none of whom is sure whether to accept his share of the largesse, especially from a man with a red nose riding a wheel. But they do, after a nudge from Mom or Dad, and the clowns move on. Jolted by a strange sense of déjà vu, I almost stick out a hand to take one of the colorful orbs, and I imagine I hear someone say, Yes, take it, take it, and I look up to see the face of my father, unshaven and dark against the sun, smiling down at me. I suddenly realize that parades are not for children at all, but for parents and grandparents—no one dies, life goes on . . . .

Here come the horses, Ben! He sits up straighter; the tip of his tail wags in greeting. They are ridden by men in western garb and now it's my turn to smile: there was a time when I wanted to be a cowboy. One of the beautiful palominos, contrary to plan, defecates right in front of us. A few embarrassed chuckles follow, but the best is yet to come: a trumpeter in the boy scout band, doing his best with a Sousa march, slips and falls in the pile of lumpy manure. Parents and children and band members laugh heartily; the laughter changes to applause when he jumps up and marches on without missing a note.

The parade ends magnificently with a huge fire engine, whose siren moves Ben to perform his famous dervish routine, to the delight of the crowd. But one or two of the kids, unmindful of Ben's antics, or anyone else's, never take their wide eyes from the sandy-haired firefighter at the big steering wheel in back of the truck, nor does he from theirs. He may be six feet tall and weigh as much as a lineman, but on that high perch sits a small boy whose dream has come true, and they know it.

32

MIRRORS

On the sidewalk outside the deli Ben and a pair of poodles wait with worried looks on their faces. Behind them a lovely young woman checks her makeup in the side mirror of a battered car. I cannot see her face, only the hopeful image in the glass, which reminds me of Allie at the fair. She is combing her shiny black hair in the reflection of the mirrored wall enclosing one of the side shows. One memory leads to another: I see her running happily toward me holding aloft a beautiful hero sandwich; she stumbles, loses control, and it springs end over end, in superslow motion, into the dirt. She pretends it doesn't matter, but I know otherwise.

Satisfied with her appearance, the Allie manquée marches off to whatever destiny she has created for herself. We proceed slowly to our own: lunch on our favorite bench.

As Ben sits at my feet waiting for a handout I notice for the first time (perhaps I am thinking about the lovely Pollyanna in the mirror) how the entire park is reflected in his big, dark eyes, one on me, the other on the potato chips. Surprised and fascinated, I see tiny people criss-cross behind me, the forest of trees, the blaring taxis rushing by in the street beyond. Curved, like the mirrors put up in dark corridors to reveal whoever might be lurking around the corner, his eyes display a panoramic view of everything. They are so clear that the smallest details can be distinguished, even the half-dozen chess players, oblivious to the outside world, banging away at my left. I can see the sky there, too, and out of it a pair of pigeons swoop down and land somewhere in the grass between the restrooms and the skateboard mound.

A man holding a little girl by the hand passes by. I hear the child spout something I cannot understand, but the voice is beautiful, if doleful, like that of an oboe. After they have swung around and disappeared in the corners of his eyes, Mabel comes into view pushing her postal cart in the opposite direction, going nowhere. She is followed by a young couple, arm in arm. A drug seller appears, and I hear the familiar, "Smoke? Smoke? Smoke and coke?" All of this is reflected in the mirrors of Ben's gentle soul.

Once, when I was a little boy, I sneaked out of the house and spent the night sitting on the riverbank studying the reflections of the stars in the twinkling water. It was so quiet I could hear insects breathing, or so I thought, and I felt so much a part of it and of everything that for one brief, exquisite moment I was sure I saw the face of God mirrored in that lucent stream.

I will probably never know what I saw on that silent night more than a decade ago. But whatever it was I have found it again in Ben's clear, luminous eyes.

33

THE MONGREL

Look, Ben, there's the brown dog! We have seen him before, do you remember? How skinny he is—you can count all of his ribs, and his feet seem to be too big for his body. Where has he been, do you suppose?

Ben, who is interested in the activities of everyone, watches closely as the mongrel scurries from one trash can to another, careful not to allow anyone to get too close to him. Perhaps he is on to the tricks of the dogcatchers; in any case he is wise enough not to turn over every receptacle he encounters, only those promising a bite of food. When he has made his selection he places his front paws on the rim and tips the can over quickly, with a minimum of noise. In seconds he has gobbled down a pizza crust and scarfed up the residue stuck to the bottom of an aluminum foil pan and is on his way before anyone can make a fuss.

I wish we could do something for him, Ben, but he would not accept our help. His education has made him apprehensive and suspicious. No one should have to live that way, my friend, neither man, nor dog, nor anyone.

The mongrel investigates a few more bins before leaving the park in the middle of the block. Though he looks in all directions he doesn't see the bagel truck bearing down on him until it is too late. I try to shout, to warn him, but all I can think of is: "Richard! Be careful!"

The driver stops and jumps from the open cab. When he sees the dead dog under his truck he jerks his head nearly 180 degrees and mutters something bitter to himself, or to God. Following this brief malediction he gently lifts the nearly weightless body by its legs and dumps it onto the sparse grass just inside the park. He climbs back into his truck and pulls away slowly, as if wary of skinny dogs leaping out from every bush. Several pedestrians hurry by the late mongrel with hardly a glance, except for one young woman, who cries over and over, "Oh, gee! Oh, gee! Oh, gee!"

Ben, who knows and understands, wants to go over and pay his final respects. When I acquiesce he licks my hand and we make our way to the park's edge to officiate at the services for the nameless mutt, who, for the first time in its miserable life, is neither terrified nor hungry.

Tonight I will give Ben two whole cans of food with no dry mixed in, and, after that, I shall hold on to him as tightly as he can stand.

34

BASKETBALL

Every afternoon, on the cement court a block from the pizza parlor, the city's Johnsons, Jordans, and Jabbars gather to show their skills. Sometimes, when we are not too eager to get to the Korean grocery for lunch, we watch for a while, caught up in the clamor and excitement and the beat of a nearby boom box.

Though it is a warm day the players sweat their way up and down the cracked concrete at tremendous speed, their bare chests rising and falling like those of the pigeons picking at a fallen sandwich on the nearby curb.

The small crowd of onlookers murmur approval or dismay at every shot, placing their own hopes and dreams in the hands of these amateur athletes in street shoes, whose frustration in spending their young adult lives in a nameless outdoor arena shows in their solemn faces as they try to prove, to themselves as well as the spectators, that they are somebody. There is no laughter here, only grunts and curses. How tragic it is, Ben, that these talented young men, who could do almost anything they put their minds to, are compelled to waste their best years throwing basketballs at netless rims.

Yet what alternatives are offered to lure them from the court? Should they hurry with bulging briefcases to the crowded subway stations, spend their days producing another bottle of hair spray, selling grosses of paper clips or cans of paint, their ghetto blasters assuring them it's all RIGHT, it's all RIGHT, it's all RIGHT . . . .

35

The Storm

The mid-June heat wave has been nearly intolerable even for Ben, who is generally indifferent to extremes of temperature, undismayed by rain or snow. But the rumble of distant thunder brings a promise of relief along with flashes of childhood. How well I remember my mother's face, white with fright whenever heavy black clouds shut out the slanted sunlight, as she scurried around the house pulling the plugs from all the electrical outlets. I can almost feel her involuntary little jumps with every flash of lightning, her agony as she waited for the crack of thunder. It was hard to know which she feared most—thunderstorms or cancer.

My brother Chris doesn't yet worry about dread disease, as far as I know, but he has inherited his mother's terror of storms, and no amount of reassurance or logic can persuade him otherwise. At the first rumble of thunder he would come running to me and, regardless of who was around or what I was doing, climb into my lap or wrap himself around my leg.

Ben sniffs and sniffs the already cooler air, testing it for clues. Perhaps he can smell the elephant man, whose feet are encrusted by a malodorous colony of fungus, sleeping off his nightly drunk on the sidewalk down the street. Lightning, followed by a loud clap! And my brave friend, who rarely shows any sign of fear, leaps onto my face and refuses to get off. Whining pathetically he pins me down; I can hardly breathe. I try to roll over for air. My can of office supplies—pencils, rubber bands, a broken ruler—goes flying, but he does not budge, and there we remain until the danger has passed.

So, Ben, you are only human! Like each of us, you, too, have your secret fears, your ghosts and demons. Don't be ashamed, my friend, for I love you all the more for them!

36

THE BAT

In the shadow of Garibaldi a man performs the slow, silent movements of the t'ai chi ch'uan. From somewhere outside the park waft wonderful hints of garlic, incense, and honey-roasted peanuts. The apricot sky is suddenly blackened by the cough of a tall smokestack hacking out its foul effluvium, violently but quickly, as if hoping no one will notice.

Ben, look—there's a bat! Where do you suppose it came from and where is it going? There aren't many flying insects in the city; it must have been a pet who got away or was evicted, just as we were. And, like us, it seems to be searching for something that may not exist. We can only hope it will find its way home again, or at least locate some peaceful sanctuary.

How beautiful! See how it swoops out of the sky, maneuvers in and around the trees, turns abruptly and climbs away, as agile as a hawk, though it is nearly blind. Are you able to hear the high-pitched sounds it uses for navigation, my friend?

Mabel is terrified. Afraid to stay put and afraid to run, she lifts her arms over her head and screams and screams, attracting little attention or sympathy from passersby. Ben whines, pleads with me to let him go over. I lift his rope over his massive head and he lumbers off in her direction. It occurs to me as I follow his lead that the bat may be sick, even rabid, which might also explain its unwonted presence in the city. Yet it seems perfectly healthy as it flits across the park in search of gnats and mosquitoes, as surprised as I was, perhaps, not to find many here. I'm afraid it will starve unless it finds its way home.

Ben has flattened himself against Mabel, whose stubby, flailing hands have found his raggedy coat. She kneels and buries her beautiful brown face in it, quiet for now. The bat, meanwhile, after making one last pass, has disappeared from sight, and I know we shall not see it again. Its appearance was a rare and wonderful occurrence, albeit a brief one, like that of everyone who enters one's life. We are all bats in the city; regardless of the duration of our stay in this world we are mere transients—here one minute, gone the next.

37

The Sun

I remember seeing, when I was a boy, a movie in which a slender ray of sunlight illuminated the site where a great treasure was buried—but only at sunset on the summer solstice. The blinding light reflected from the massive cache of hammered gold, unearthed after untold centuries, could be seen for miles.

This hot afternoon is much like that brilliant day. The intensity of the late-afternoon sun emboldens and, yes, sanctifies everything it touches this hour: the vibrant young trees at the corner of the park, the slate roofs of the mews, Vincent's shimmering canvas, even the pocked cement under our feet.

The chess players, too, are ennobled by the magnificent radiance, and every move seems directed by God. At the same time it is strangely quiet, the opulent atmosphere having struck a harmonic chord not only in the participants, but in kibitzers and passersby alike. Perhaps they are recalling, if unconsciously, some romantic beach or holy place, just as I remember Allie laughing in her lavender swimsuit, Chris streaking down the slippery slide and splashing into the pool.

How unreal it all is! The world seems magnified, bigger than life! Everything and everyone, even the vagrants and the pushers, have become splendid, almost angelic, in the empyrean light, which turns the windows in the big office buildings to silver and the rusty water towers to deep wells of shining copper. How serene Otto looks this hour, how stately the pretzel man, how brave the pigeons! And my beloved Ben, already priceless, has become a burnished ingot of purest gold.

38

Pavarotti

We are awakened by a rat looking for something to eat and finding only Ben and me. Ben's ears twitch as he watches it forage in the corner by my right foot. The light is too dim to see what color it is, but it is small, probably less than full-grown. It doesn't seem to notice us.

Ben is distracted by something else. He lifts his head and studies our concrete ceiling. His good ear points straight up, like a steeple, and his nostrils expand and dilate, expand and dilate. The rat directs his tiny nose skyward also. I try vainly to pick up whatever it is that has come to the attention of all the sentient creatures in the vicinity except myself.

Then I hear it: a faraway singer is serenading the empty street with an aria from a great opera. The music grows louder and louder, interrupted every few minutes by an irate resident: "Shut up! People are trying to sleep here!" Once or twice I hear a missile clatter to the pavement. It is all very Chaplinesque.

But nothing fazes the local Pavarotti, whose musical dreams cannot be dashed by mere sticks and stones. Like a pair of sunflowers clocking the day, the heads of Ben and the rat follow the unseen tenor as he approaches and then treads unevenly above us. "Shut up, you!" from the hard-smoking woman across the street, though it sounds only half-serious, as if she couldn't sleep anyway. The clomping and the singing stop immediately and there is a disturbing silence, an uncomfortable pause. Ben and the rat, their heads still pointed straight up, listen intently. Through the bars of the wrought-iron gate a stream of urine suddenly rushes, spattering down the steps and onto the little sidewalk in front of us. When it is over, the song begins again right where it was interrupted, and the neighborhood exhales, secretly relieved that all is well and the threads of life and time have not been broken for now. "Shut the fuck up!" from the hardhat a few doors down, but there aren't any teeth in it.

The animals in my company continue to follow the music as it fades in the west, their ears still tuned in long after I can no longer hear it. I imagine all the people above us in their beds, their ears twitching, wondering whether anyone actually came by at all, and why they feel vaguely melancholy.

The rat scurries around at my feet and, finding nothing to eat, disappears through a crack in the cement to seek his meager repast on the street. Ben yawns, rests his head on my stomach. His ears are still in motion, hearing things I never shall. He seems to be thinking—about the rat, perhaps, wondering if it had really been there, yet feeling the anguish of its bitter existence.

39

THE BANGER

No matter how cold or rainy it is there are always a few chess players at the corner tables in the park. Ben and I sometimes watch a game or two, not because the strategies are brilliant (though I suspect they are), but because we are drawn in by the fervor and intensity.

Most of the frowning competitors are frequent participants with familiar faces. Many are playing for money, but it doesn't seem to make much difference in the quality of the games: the amateurs are just as caught up in their little world of knights and bishops as are the pros and con artists.

One of the regulars is unbeatable. The others call him "The Banger" because of his habit of smashing down the timer button after each move, accompanied by his own superfluous "Bang!" You can hear him all over the park. This and his general impatience (he twitches and snorts and clears his throat constantly) agitate and unnerve his opponents as much as does his formidable ability. His table is always surrounded by a battery of murmuring kibitzers, whom he ignores. Like the pigeon man, he seems to weigh almost nothing.

His ebony face is a moonscape of dents and scars said to have been inflicted by sore losers, but that may be part of the mystique. Another rumor has it that he once killed a man, and spent most of his life in the state prison. Yet, he never suffers from a lack of challengers: every player around wants to be the one who beat The Banger.

His responses are astonishingly quick; he seems to anticipate his opponent's every move and "Bang!" The onlookers smile, scratch their chins, wag their heads. Today's victim, a math professor wearing a long ponytail, remains outwardly calm, but his darting eyes give him away. His tactics are a shambles, his overall strategy forgotten. He is shaken, his confidence gone.

In no more than thirty moves it is over. The Banger leaps to his feet, thrusts out a hand. Not to clasp the loser's but to collect his winnings. He bows solemnly to the crowd, who applaud appreciatively, and hurries to the crack house a few blocks away. On his way past us he touches Ben on the head and gets a wag. He nods at me also, and I dismally return it. I have never seen such a battered face, or eyes carrying such pain and torment.

We watch him leave the park on the run. Ben whines, and so do I. The eyes of the kibitzers follow him too. In the game of life the Banger was checkmated long, long ago.

40

The Wedding

A man in a threadbare black suit tails a young couple across the park. They offer him money, but he doesn't want it—it is souls he is after. Shouting passages from the Bible he follows them out of the park and around the corner.

From the church across the street a bride and groom erupt. They fly down the steps as if afraid of being drenched by the brief shower of rice. But their haste has more to do with their eagerness to begin their new life together—don't you think, Ben?—a desire once shared by Allie and me.

For a wonderful moment I put myself in the groom's shiny new shoes, running the gauntlet of aunts and uncles to the toilet paper-covered Honda and (I imagine) the coastal Maine honeymoon. We arrive at the little cabin late in the evening; someone has already built a fire in the fireplace. How fragrant the piney smoke rising straight to heaven! I've always thought it to be the aroma of perfect happiness and contentment, haven't you, my friend? But of course you associate all smells with happiness, don't you?

Have I ever told you about Allie, Ben? Her hair is as black and shiny as a raven, her teeth as white as the newly-fallen snow that you love so well. She has a beautiful voice and sweet breath, like the breezes along the river....

In the unlikely event that the newlyweds were to ask what advice I would give them as they begin their marriage, I would tell them this: take your happiness while you can, even if you know it won't last forever—the chance may never come again! But they won't ask me, or anyone, nor should they. You have to learn such things for yourself.

There they go, my friend, accompanied by the clattering of beer cans, to wherever their lives take them. Let's wish them perfect happiness and contentment, shall we?

Godspeed! Godspeed!

41

CRI DE COEUR

The colorful birds of summer—the older students who come to learn new skills or to re-learn unused or forgotten ones—have returned to try to recapture elusive youth. It is the season of brief liaisons, those sweet, strong attachments which live in secret, nighttime memory until the end of time. One can see them on the park benches or at the sidewalk cafés, holding hands and brushing knees: lifetimes telescoped into moments, seconds which must last forever.

One of these short-term visitors prances into the park. She is a beautiful platinum blonde, well-groomed and frisky, and she heads straight for Ben, whose left eye follows her approach with mounting interest, the other gazing up at me. Unable to suppress his impatience he finally leaps to his feet. His tail swings so violently that it could break an unwary leg; I jump quickly out of the way. Some guttural moan I have not heard before emanates from deep inside his chest.

The lovely young Komondor draws nearer and nearer. Ben, awash in anticipation, quaffs her pheromones drunkenly, unashamedly. His sense of anticipation is terrible. He can't stand still. Only a dozen yards separate them now, and even that distance diminishes systematically. An adolescence of dreaming and waiting is over.

But her guardian, as if noticing Ben and me for the first time, pulls hard on her leash and continues past us without a word or second look. Ben can't believe this and neither can the Komondor, who receives a nasty jerk each time she looks back at him. I, in the meantime, hold tightly to his rope. Long after they have gone he finally stops straining, though he continues to whine softly through the rest of the sad afternoon.

I explain to him that life is unpredictable, irreversible, unfair and all the rest, but he doesn't want to hear it. He won't touch his supper, a handful of dry food mixed with a dropped or discarded hamburger. Though he is no longer whining, his eyes and nostrils, searching for signs of her return, are never still. When, at last, it is time to leave, he lopes to where she has been, takes a final deep whiff of her mysterious essence, and lets out a long, miserable wail, one that she will surely hear and understand. I don't know whether she does or not, but I do, and I join him in a pitiful duet.

42

NATIONAL HOLIDAY

As we lean comfortably against the barricade between the quay and the noisy highway, Ben sniffs the warm night air constantly, expectantly.

The great fiery sun has just set behind the blackened skyline across the river, and the clouds have become gentle red sheep. All around us thousands of our fellow citizens have gathered to celebrate whatever freedoms they hold dear. The mood is lighthearted, anticipatory. I, too, can hardly wait for the pyrotechnics to begin. A fireworks display is much like a parade, each very like the one that came before, the familiar noise and bluster creating the happy illusion that nothing ever changes.

   A muffled pop, a cheer, and the first firecracker rises softly into the velveteen sky. Hundreds of eyes, including Ben's and mine, follow it up and up until it gently explodes high over the river, sending tiny flares of sparkling reds and whites and blues in every direction. The crowd applauds and Ben lights up in a ghostly aura of pink and purple. Unaware of his colorful glow, he watches me somewhat apprehensively with a reflecting eye.

   Another fuzzy missile rises and, exactly at its apex, bursts into a flowery orange Roman candle whose shimmering petals drift slowly, slowly to the black water below. Its sad beauty reminds me of the display Chris and I went to a year ago. How he clung to me beneath all the noise and glare! I close my eyes and can almost feel his frail little body next to mine. I find myself wishing with all my heart that he were here.

   Suddenly there is an unexpectedly bright flash and, after a second or two, the earsplitting bang of a heavenly cannonball. Ben immediately throws himself against my chest, flattening me against the cement wall. It is all I can do to squirm out from under him and get to my feet. Still he presses against me with his entire weight, which seems to have tripled, and he begs to go home, or anywhere, out of the storm.

   I wrap my arms around him hoping that, back at Grandma's, someone is hugging Chris tight, whispering in his ear, telling him to hush, hush, it will all be over soon.

43

Drinking Buddies

On the way to the church to hold the door for the pious this warm Sunday morning, we come across a drunk curled up on the sidewalk, his bare, swollen feet protruding into the gutter. He is lying on his side with his pants pulled down as if to moon all of humanity, but, in fact, it is to cool a burning rash running from top to bottom of his backside. He smells of urine and a long drool streams from his encrusted lips. As revolting a sight as he is, I nonetheless take a good look at his face to make sure he isn't my father. Ben, in the meantime, sniffs and whines, sniffs and whines.

Would you like to hear about my old man, Ben? Until my mother died, Dad was a Friday night drinker who sometimes spent or lost his whole paycheck in a bar. When I was old enough it became my duty to go find him, to bring home his wallet if I could, or at least enough money for groceries. I hated that job, but he hated it even more because it embarrassed him in front of his friends.

He began to conjure up ways to elude my searches, like going into a tavern I had just left. After I got onto that scheme he would simply buy a couple of bottles and take them to the river or the railroad tracks and drink alone. I imagine he hated that too, and I suppose he hated me; he called me his "rotten little spy." Yet, like most alcoholics, he was a wonderful man when he was sober: kind, gentle, and generous. Like you, my friend.

Then he began to drink more regularly, with briefer and briefer periods on the wagon. He became moody and depressed even when he was sober, though he was never a mean drunk. After that, the only time he quit for any length of time was when Mom was dying of cancer. As soon as she was gone he went straight to a bar. He never even made it to the funeral, Ben, and I rarely saw him sober after that. But maybe it wasn't all his fault. No one is perfect, my friend, not even you.

Should we say a prayer for my father when we get to the church today, and for all alcoholics everywhere? Do you think it would do any good? Or, if there is a God, has He already condemned them to the deepest corners of hell, where there is never a moment of comfort or peace? If it's too much to ask of Him, my friend, let's close our eyes and imagine my poor father sleeping soundly in a bed somewhere on this bright, sunny morning, with nice clean clothes and a good pair of shoes to put on when he wakes up.

44

STARS

A young man wearing green leather shorts hurries along the diagonal sidewalk jerk-jerk-jerking a mixed-breed terrier who tries vainly to stop and sniff this or that outcropping. Most of the other students and faculty are watching TV somewhere, or sitting in one of the countless bars or coffee houses, and the park is quiet except for an angry schizophrenic shouting about some long-remembered injustice. The malediction awakens another vagrant, who had been sleeping upright on a bench, a single carnation protruding from his thin, interlocked hands. He raises up, farts long and loudly, settles down again.

They will be closing the park soon. I free Ben for one last patrol over the territory of his elusive nemeses, the squirrels, which he undertakes with his usual relish. But Blackie and the others have retired for the night and their smaller relatives have not yet made their nocturnal appearances. The nearly full moon is already up; I squint to bring in a star, but it is only a distant airplane.

Even without starlight the city is beautiful at dusk. The tall buildings with their irregular pattern of luminous windows, the vibrant yellow gleam of the mercury lights, and the softer glow of the old-fashioned street lamps all generate an aura of well-being that permeates the still, warm air. The taxis spray their bouncing beams here and there, as if flushing out trade from the trees and bushes. A silent police car whizzes by, flashing its brilliant red-white-red-white, instilling mystery and excitement into the otherwise peaceful proceedings.

To the east the pink and blue neon lights of the pharmacy and the dry cleaning establishment add color to the spectacle, and the bright reflecting shirt and shoes of a dedicated jogger circling the park produce brief, regular twinkles, like the signals of a nearby pulsar. And underlying everything, like the background radiation of the universe, hums the permanent urban glow. The city is a firmament unto itself.

There's a rat, looking for a pretzel crumb the pigeons missed, an unfinished hot dog. "Wha' fo'?" yells the schizo. "Fuck dat shit!"

C'mon, Ben, it's time to go home.

45

NIGHT LIFE

Somewhere a dog howls. Ben, who has been dancing in his dreams, pops awake. He listens intently for a moment, whines, sighs loudly. Perhaps he is thinking of the unattainable Komondor.

Unable to sleep, I get up and empty my urinal into the gutter, marking my territory, claiming the broken curb as my own. Ben, also restive, wants to walk, and we take to the midnight streets in search of cool breezes and peace of mind. My furry companion, excited by the prospect of nocturnal adventure, snuffles and snorts at every sidewalk singularity, staking his own claims to every pole and hydrant.

A man sitting at the bottom of a stoop demands a cigarette. He is stripped to the waist and his feet are bare. When I confess that I don't smoke he shrugs and offers me a swig from a huge bottle of beer. I decline, but Ben, who never waits for an invitation, laps the dewy condensation from the cool brown magnum. In the window a yellow cat, like the one who sits in the doorway of the cobbler's shop, watches Ben with studied calm.

Farther down the street a rat meanders aimlessly along the curb. Ben follows its unhurried movements with considerable interest until a faraway siren breaks his concentration and prods him into a halfhearted whirl. The lethargic rodent, meanwhile, disappears down a hole in the gutter.

A few steps away a cockroach appears, but it, too, loafs along, as if trying to avoid heatstroke. Did you know, my attentive friend, that these animals are wonderful parents? Maybe even better than you would be, for dogs are notorious rakes. Certainly better than a lot of people I know. They're smarter than we are, too. It has been said that when the Earth becomes uninhabitable for people and even dogs, the cockroaches will still find it a paradise.

Ben—look! The gate to the courtyard of the big apartment complex is ajar, and the guard can't see the fountain from his post. Let's have a cool dip in the rainbow-colored water, then an indulgent roll in the thick green grass!

46

TRASH 'N' TREASURE

It seems, on this wonderfully cool, breezy, late afternoon, that every trash can has its patron, every dumpster its client. Most of the park's habitués are completing their day's rounds, rummaging for bottles and cans, food and clothing, while there is still light. Some are pushing shopping carts or shouldering large black plastic bags to which a useful item—a salable book or magazine, a sweater with a tiny hole in the armpit, a vial of aspirin—is infrequently added. The more valuable commodities—the contents of a styrofoam food carton, a pair of close-fitting shoes, a beer bottle with a finger or two left in it—are consumed on the spot. It all reminds me of the antique store Allie used to like to visit, a place called "Trash 'n' Treasure," where she poked around for valuables among the dusty scrap, sometimes picking up an old bauble or utensil, connecting the past to the future, she would tell me.

On rare occasions a gem is found buried under the park's rubble. Last winter I saw a wino pull a twenty-dollar bill from the depths of a trash can. He was so excited that he ran off without his grocery cart (which he would need again as soon as the money ran out), leaving him with a net loss for the transaction. Another lucky bum took it over and he, in turn, left his rickety little wagon for the next browser to find, a sort of pauperized trickle-down economics.

Ben and I, who are addicted only to sunshine and pleasant dreams, and who need only food to survive, rarely attend these valuable leavings unless we have been caught in the rain without an umbrella. Surprisingly, others with far greater means than we are sometimes less finicky. The psychologists would be amazed, for example, to discover how many lawyers and brokers pilfer their daily newspapers from containers laced with excrement and other odious deposits.

Look, Ben, there's the man with no feet, who has somehow made it through another day. And Mabel, who is remarkably adept at fishing blankets and clothing from the bottom of the dumpsters behind the public toilets. To many of those hurrying through the park on their way to cool apartments or restaurants or theaters, we who are homeless are a kind of garbage ourselves. A year ago I might have thought the same. But that was before I looked into the eyes of Otto, Mabel, the Banger.

Who is to say which of us is trash and which is treasure? Don't you wish, my friend, that everyone felt as you do, that each of us is something to cherish, and well worth saving?

47

THE MAGIC DWARF

A woman with a silver ring in her nose speeds by, a parrot perched on her left shoulder. He is as colorful as the evanescent rainbow we caught a glimpse of in yesterday's gentle mist. "Pieces of shit!" the bird squawks. "Pieces of shit!" They are followed by a man admonishing an undaunted toy dog: "You *know* we don't do things like that, Clarence! You *know* that!"

In the middle of the park a modern-day Merlin is setting up shop. From a small blue suitcase he pulls a top hat, a wand, an aubergine silk handkerchief. Without ado of any kind, the performance begins. Ben and I amble over for a closer look—who can resist the antics and possibilities of a magician?

While a sparse crowd begins to gather, the diminutive sorcerer, demonstrating deft co-ordination and practiced showmanship, entertains us with card tricks and dwarf jokes. His stubby fingers render astonishing feats with aces and jacks, and the laughter of the small audience brings a few more passersby to a halt, though most hurry on by, oblivious to anything extraordinary they might encounter along the pathways of their already supersaturated lives.

Now that he has the full attention of a quorum he proceeds in earnest. The cards and handkerchief disappear (up a sleeve?), the top hat becomes a contribution basket. With great seriousness and obvious strength of character he slowly scans the crowd, making eye contact with each of us, even Ben. His face, too lined for its age, breaks into a beatific smile, and he announces in a nasal, high-pitched voice: "If I can catch a flying pigeon within the next ten minutes your fondest dream will come true." Those of us gathered around the makeshift table shift our feet uncertainly. The revival of long-discarded hopes sounds wonderful, but who can catch a pigeon? Just in case, however, I formulate a silent, heartfelt wish.

Totally absorbed, we watch the magician raise his wand and clamp it between yellow, horse-like teeth. Then he freezes, as do we all. No one moves or speaks. A minute passes, two, five. A few non-believers depart without a word or a contribution to the hat. The rest of us contemplate our lives, intrigued, I suspect, by the chance, however remote, of a miracle: a caught pigeon, a new-found love. Nine minutes. Throats are cleared.

Suddenly a bird materializes out of nowhere, circles, circles, alights on the wand. Slowly the magician raises his arms and grasps the beautiful speckled pigeon in his plump, delicate hands. The crowd is utterly silent for a moment, then breaks out into spontaneous applause. The dwarf bows and immediately releases the pigeon, who flies away, out of the park.

Mass hypnosis? A trained bird? Who knows? But the hat fills with bills, the would-be Merlin folds his little table, and a dozen inspired people fan out with renewed determination to give life another try. If that isn't magic, my furry friend, then the stars are pinholes in a cardboard sky.

48

Summer Heat

In the church across the street someone is practicing the bass part of an organ piece, whose heavy tones add their weight to the already viscous air. The early afternoon sun radiates down on the motionless park like a visible roar. An hour ago, at precisely 12:18 p.m., when we left to pick up our lunch at the Korean grocery and deli, the digital thermometer at the savings and loan declared a temperature of 92°F (33°C), and it is probably even hotter now. The sun is a haloed white ingot high in the thick, powder-blue sky, and the pigeons and squirrels have retreated from its penetrating light. There are few passersby at our bench, and they move along only slowly, with measured steps, as if terminally ill.

Ben lies sleeping at my feet in the shade of the sycamore tree, his gentle snoring the only sound under the sky's hot breath. The relentless luminescence creeps slowly toward him, like a predatory beast, peering under every brilliant leaf and white-hot stone. Finally it reaches his wet, ebony nose, now dry, gray, and minutely cracked, a tiny flaring desert. Slowly it inches up his snout, which immediately becomes dry and yellowish under its harsh gaze, like a pile of discarded straw. I fidget for his sake, but Ben doesn't move. The incandescent light slowly creeps past his twitching ears, and still he does not budge: perhaps he is dreaming of a frozen winter dawn or a gulp of raspberry slush.

The burning rays inch along his body, a hairy orange clock, as inexorably as time itself. At his chest a famous actor dies, at the navel a bridge collapses. A symphony is completed at his left hock. At last he lies completely encircled by the broad spotlight of the sun. He stirs, finally, but it is only to gaze up at me with an expression I have seen before—when he has finished a wonderful scratch or is resting after a hearty supper or a long run with Fricka and the others—the one which contends: "Isn't it wonderful?" Ah, Ben. You never forget, do you, the source of your life, of all life.

49

Olympic Skaters

A red squirrel digs up an acorn and eats it with quick, sharp bites, disregarding the dead rat lying nearby. Ben, his eyes fixated on a pair of slow-moving pigeons, ignores them both.

A man shouting epithets to himself walks his dog past the boisterous playground. The well-groomed cocker spaniel pays no attention whatever to his ranting and, indeed, seems quite content with her lot. I guess one can get used to almost anything, Ben....

A pair of roller bladers, ages eight or nine, skate around and around the cement circle at the heart of the park. Despite their tender years they are quite accomplished, if charmingly awkward, and a sizable crowd has gathered to urge them on. They are dressed in glittering outfits—perhaps they are rehearsing for some important juvenile event. Like the basketball players over near the pizza parlor they are serious about their sport: there are no smiles, no youthful chatter. But this is not the hopeless clawing at what might have been; it is the surefootedness of knowing what will come. The spectators, caught up in the gravity of it all, remain silent also, save the occasional "Ooh!", the scattered applause.

We, too, understand the excitement of the possible, and step up to catch a glimpse of the future. Look at them fly, Ben, see how effortless they make it seem! At the same time, the performance is somehow humbling. All of us regardless of age or station, secretly chastise ourselves for not having done more with our lives, for not having achieved our highest capabilities.

But I can't remember ever wanting anything so badly as these determined kids aspire to be the best. Look at their faces! They are willing to work and work for it. Yet, even that is not enough, I think. There is an elusive and indefinable quality, usually called "heart," an attribute which you possess in abundance, my friend, that lifts the champion from the depths of defeat and compels him to go on and on and on. Only time will tell whether these pre-adolescents share that attribute in sufficient measure.

A sudden gasp from the crowd: the skaters, trying to stretch their limits, have fallen. The girl is crying. A young woman, perhaps a mother or coach, starts toward them. But her companion holds her back. The boy, who seems astonished at finding himself on the ground, finally climbs to his feet and skates over to help his partner to hers. Another tragedy! In attempting to rise, they fall again, together in a heap. After a synchronous intake of breath the crowd remains silent, expectant. This time the boy laughs, then the girl. Oblivious to the rest of us they heartily enjoy their semi-private joke for a minute or two before pulling themselves up to begin all over again, right from the top.

I think they're going to make it, Ben!

50

COURAGE

From time to time the man with no feet takes up his station at the southeast corner of the park, his knobby stumps graphically exposed in order to generate pity and funding for his next binge. In between these brief appearances he vanishes, sometimes for weeks, to have his legs shortened still further. Like a grim Cheshire cat he is slowly disappearing, an inch at a time, and one day there will be nothing left but a sardonic scowl.

I am always surprised when he turns up again, and saddened, too. Yet, buoyed, somehow, by the ferocious tenacity, his persistent clinging to what little life he has left. I never fail to wonder whether my father has done as well, whether he has managed to survive, whether he still has feet.

How different the old woman with the red-rimmed eyes who traverses the park almost daily, on, one would think, an unavoidable errand. It is painfully obvious how difficult the expedition is for her. She progresses with the help of a pair of canes and a bright green backpack, a giant upright turtle on artificial limbs. Every few steps she stops to rest; her journey across the park takes upwards of fifteen minutes. Yet her bearing is dignified, her expression serene. As she struggles toward us I see beneath the ancient carapace a young girl who married the boy next door, sacrificing her own wants and desires to raise a happy family, now grown and gone away, having left her behind like some outmoded appliance. Her courage, like that of the man with no feet, is profoundly moving—not only because of her personal bravery but also because she somehow represents all those who have to get through life's parks day after day on their own weak limbs, their only crutch a bottle, a joint, a dirty needle.

51

LIFE AND DEATH

An ambulance appears in the night, quietly, whispering of death. It has come for the old woman across the street. Unable to sleep, I perch on one of the trash cans to watch. Ben, perhaps realizing that nothing can be done, dozes on.

There is no hurry to take her anywhere, and the attendants drain their paper cups before climbing the stoop and going inside. When the door is opened for them they are greeted by the sound of a baby crying.

It was only this morning that we spotted our scrawny neighbor wheezing down the other side of the street with her last bag of canned soups and TV dinners and cigarettes. She didn't return my wave, but I thought I caught a hint of a smile, which made her look twenty years younger. Her demeanor reminded me of my mother's just before she died, when the pain and fear had been transcended and she was actually looking forward, I believe, to her appointment with St. Peter (though she was still afraid of tornadoes). Perhaps Mom, or someone, was there to escort the old woman through the portals of death, to show her the way.

Ben awakens at the first sound of commotion: they are bringing out the covered body on a stretcher. His great head rises, his good ear comes up, he sniffs the air. Though he whines a final farewell it is similar to the sound he makes when I open a can of food for him.

They lift her remains into the ambulance. There is some discussion with a relative or friend—about her temporary location, I suppose—and the vehicle pulls away, as slowly and silently as it came. The baby stops crying and the street is quiet, as if deep in thought. Wondering who will be next, possibly, or whether affairs are in order. Do you know what my father told me once when he was sober, Ben? He said, "Try not to live as if you were going to die some day, but as if you will live forever . . . ."

No, my big orange friend, death is nothing to fear. It is life that requires grit, someone to show us the way.

52

REBIRTH

The run is already a circus of activity when we arrive—Alexander the Great Dane trying to mount the beautiful young mastiff, Diana; Duke picking a fight with little Luna; others chasing chartreuse tennis balls, sticks, each other.

There is a new dog here this morning—a Weimaraner who looks so much like Fricka that Ben does a bona fide double-take. Then we see the broadly smiling Chinese woman: it *is* Fricka, a phoenix risen from the ashes of her beloved predecessor.

Owing to youth and unfamiliarity with her surroundings the pup is more timid than her namesake, though nonetheless adventuresome, and when Ben tries to roll her over she responds by returning the compliment. It is clear that they are going to be great friends.

When her guardian spots Ben she runs over to shake my hand. She is the happiest person I have seen in a long time—Christmas-morning, Easter-egg, Halloween-candy joyful—bursting to talk about her family, her new apartment, and about Fricka II, who has discovered Ben's (Fricka I's) rubber newspaper and is running all over the lot with it, Ben loping after her baretoothed, feigning rage. She was only hours away from dog pound death when her new companion arrived to claim her. Why she chose that particular day to search for another dog is a complete mystery to my beaming confidant. "Something just tell me to go to pound," she explains. "Fricka is only Weimaraner they have." I, to whom everything is a mystery, am not surprised by this revelation. Ben, after all, came from nowhere, too.

I tell her my name. "I am Sung Tieng," she responds, then looks away at once. But we have made contact. For a brief moment we have overcome the fear and inhibition we are trained—by our parents, our schools, our paranoid society—to embrace. Side by side we watch Ben and Fricka and all the other dogs play and play.

53

Gulls

Ben loves to worry the gulls as they stand nonchalantly on the piers along the river. Although he has never caught one, or anything else, he always gives it his all—maybe this will be the day! His foolish quests always make me laugh, while his optimism reminds me that this might indeed be the morning that something wonderful happens. If he can chase birds, I can pursue dreams.

But there is only one scenario: Dad lashes himself to the wagon, Allie and I graduate, we get married, go to college. She becomes a famous interior designer, I a poet, and we have a son just like Chris . . . .

My happy lamentation is intensified by the vision of a young couple holding hands at the end of the pier, gazing at the gray water, the blanket of clouds, the stars they cannot see. They are not strangers: they are Allie and myself, eons and eons ago. I turn away, pretending I have seen nothing.

Ben, having rousted the birds to the top of the pilings, sniffs for treasures under the ruined boards below. The wind picks up and the gulls go into their well-rehearsed vaudeville routine, hanging motionless in the air, their wings outstretched, going nowhere, an act they have practiced for millions of years.

What would it be like to be a gull, Ben—a short life but a happy one, do you think? Wouldn't you love to be able to fly? To soar over the world and see everything clearly, from a different perspective? But of course you are perfectly content as you are, aren't you, my friend?

The wind calms itself temporarily and the birds settle again on the pier, their feathers ruffling in the breeze like the ripples on the water below. My slow-footed companion, seizing his opportunity, makes another gallop at them.

Go for it, Ben! This could be the day!

54

The Bible Salesman

Near our regular bench a rotund figure, toting a large cardboard box, appears. Wheezing like a beached orca he sets up a collapsible table and grunts a pile of little red Testaments onto the rickety stand. He wipes the perspiration from his face with a large white handkerchief and proceeds to hawk his wares at the students and other passersby, few of whom take him up on the free offer. When someone succumbs to his overture he tips his porkpie hat and mumbles something I cannot hear. None of the recipients replies; all hurry away wearing astonished expressions on their faces.

The obese spreader of the Word is probably in his mid-forties, though his face, which is laced with purple blotches and simplicity, maintains the innocence of a child. From time to time he inhales deeply; the slow exhalation is invariably followed by a blustery "Phew!" Whether this is a nervous habit or the manifestation of some heart or lung disease I cannot say, but Ben utters a little whine after each pathetic cycle.

My thoughts are distracted by the approach of a Spanish-speaking couple who argue loudly beneath the canopy of a large yellow umbrella, though it stopped raining nearly half an hour ago. The woman has been splashed with muddy water, and she gestures repeatedly toward her spotty attire. She blames her escort; he denies the charge. When they have made their noisy exit from the park I turn back to the Bible salesman. He is crying.

I do not know what has precipitated this cascade of tears, but the deep breaths are coming faster and he is sweating more profusely. "Phew!" he wheezes. "Phew! Phew!" Ben whines in earnest now. He wants to go over to commiserate with the fat man. I, who have not read the gospels since my mother died, follow him over to request a copy. From close up I discover that the purveyor's face is not only birthmarked but heavily pocked, like Otto's. As I take the Testament I quite expect him to exclaim "Praise Jesus!" in the thick, phlegmy voice of the fundamentalist preachers of my youth. Instead he tips his hat and blubbers, "Read it and weep, Charlie. Read it and weep." Shaken, I tug Ben away and we drift over to the far side of the park.

Looking back I see the Bible salesman mopping his brow as he waits for another taker. Even from this distance we can hear his soulful lament: "Phew! Phew!"

55

Truck Farm

In a little fenced-in patch of land behind the big grocery store, a few of the gentry have sown tiny gardens of tomatoes and cabbages, beans and carrots. Along the south end someone has planted a row of sunflowers, whose huge heads catch and absorb the life-giving rays of the sun and follow it across the hot blue sky.

The bold flowers make me feel as though I were a boy again, weeding the pickles and peas next to the horseshoe court and desuckering the endless rows of corn, which my mother canned in the hottest days of late summer, her sleeveless print dress soaked in front and back. How good that corn tasted in mid-winter, how it brought back the warmth of the garden and Mom's beautiful red face, the clank of ringers. Did I ever tell you, my friend, that my father was a champion horseshoe pitcher, one of the best in the state? I once saw him throw twenty doubles in a row—a tournament record, I think.

Some of the tomatoes are almost ripe—see them over there? I feel sorry for all the children of the city who have never sat in a forest of tomato vines with a smile and a salt shaker, don't you?

Allie and I wanted to have a house and a garden some day. But this one, behind its heavy wire fence and double-locked gate, may be the only one we ever know, my friend, and our subterranean refuge our only residence. If we ever did get back home again, here is one of the first things I would do: I would spade up the weedy ground behind the horseshoe court and plant an enormous garden. Not for me, but for you to smell and Chris to remember. Some hot August day, after we've tossed a few shoes, and you're snorting around for groundhogs and rabbits, I'm going to hand him a salt shaker and say, "Go to it, kid!" Wouldn't you love to be there, Ben?

56

Potpourri

Having saved enough for a day's meals with a few coins left over, I decide to take the morning off. It is perfect for a long walk: cloudy, cool, windless, a hint of still-distant autumn in the air. Ben, who loves to try new paths, is drunk with excitement. He lurches back and forth across the sidewalk examining a hydrant here, a stoop there, the rear tire of a battered car—the same one broken into a few weeks ago—bearing a sign taped to the window: NO RADIO— NOTHING WORTH SHIT.

At the bus stop a young woman pleads with a girlfriend, "Come with me; I don't want to go by myself!"

The fumy conveyance pulls up. It is stuffed with people who have somewhere to go. "There's noplace to set," the friend laments. "Where we gonna set?" They climb up and the bus lurches away.

A trash truck rolls by. Sitting on the hood is a dirty teddy bear with an arm and an eye missing. It is smiling, nonetheless.

A whole row of colorful and sweet-smelling stalls has sprung up overnight, like a meadow of late-summer flowers, on the street where all the furniture stores have been going out of business for months or years. Ben is excited by the abundance and variety, and his great orange snout takes in the olfactory wonder of each overladen booth. We shop early, before the crowds arrive, so that we might have unencumbered views and best selections.

If you have money and want a pair of gloves or socks, sunglasses or sweatshirts, the young man wearing white bucks has them all and more. Lamps, shades, bulbs, extension cords—the guy with the tattoos on both arms is ready to deal. Old records, books, *National Geographics* are available, by the ton, from the elderly couple and their chocolate-brown dachshund, whom Ben examines immediately for gender and disposition. For twenty-five cents we come away with well-thumbed copies of *Vanity Fair, Great Expectations, The Selected Writings of Juan Ramón Jiménez.*

Cheap watches, expensive candles, *objets d'art,* a kaleidoscope as rich and varied as life itself. Even at this early hour you can find hot sausages, knishes, funnel cakes, honey-roasted peanuts, coffee and soft drinks, purveyed by an endless assortment of weekend entrepreneurs, some of whom want to chat, while others scowl and pretend we are invisible. Although my observations on this score are limited, biased, and statistically insignificant, they nonetheless lead me to conclude that generosity of character is directly proportional to the readiness and width of a smile.

The all-pervading redolence drives me to exhaust our resources on a cookie for Ben and one for me, which come, I am pleased to discover after the fact, with a free cup of coffee. The proprietress of this nonprofitable enterprise, I note with satisfaction, is a plump, middle-aged lady bearing a big, toothy grin.

57

The Idiot

Sometimes, late in the afternoon, a tall, thin woman pushes a wheelchair across the park. Strapped into it is a teenage girl whose arms and head are never still, whose mouth never closes. When she gets to our bench the woman always stops for a moment to allow the girl to have a look at Ben and to pound his rough, shaggy coat. This never fails to elicit a yelp or blubber from the witless girl, which are expressions of delight, according to her mother. Ben, who understands both joy and tragedy, stands beside the chair stoically, unmindful of the flailing arms which grasp unceasingly at the air in search of substance and meaning.

The woman, in an unusually talkative mood, explains to me that her child was born this way for no reason at all; that is, she did not take drugs or even smoke or drink during the pregnancy. "She is an act of God, plain and simple," she declares bitterly, in her strong, sad voice. As if for emphasis she wheels the chair away at once, without a word or gesture of good-bye. Ben and I watch silently as they roll past bench after bench, none of whose occupants return the girl's violent salutations.

What do you think, my friend? Is happiness proportional to intelligence and co-ordination? I doubt it, don't you? Indeed, my vast experience in a world filled with creatures of all capabilities and sensitivities suggests just the opposite. Many otherwise intelligent people are extraordinarily morose, having spent their lives questioning, examining too closely. And who, after all, is happier than you and your friends? Perhaps it is not the severely retarded, but those of us who cannot understand the simple pleasures of life that one should pity.

There she goes past the chess tables and out of the park, her hands waving a spasmodic farewell, her soul, for all we know, bursting with joy.

58

Ambrosia

At the deli a man as destitute as we spends his only dollar on a lottery ticket. "This is the one!" he winks on his way out. The grocery is devoid of other customers now and the owner, who knows me well, takes time to chat. He always asks the same thing: "Why you on street?" When I try to explain he nods and grunts, as if comprehending what I don't understand myself. In kind, he tells me about his own family, his raison d'être. All his children will go to college—one doctor, one lawyer, one teacher, one businessman. He smiles broadly.

"One plus one plus one plus one equal one twenty-six," he proclaims. I stare back at the uneven teeth, a miniature skyline. "Seven eighteen-hour day!" he explains, and then shrieks a violent "Ho ho ho ho ho ho ho!"

When he has recovered he points to a frayed basket perched on the counter. "Excellent fruit—one dollah." The fruit is overripe but there is a lot of it; besides, I must not refuse this generous gesture. As I depart with the excellent fruit I hear him shout again, "Seven eighteen-hour day! Ho, ho, ho, ho, ho, ho, ho!"

Once in the park, Ben and I examine the windfall. There is only one rotten orange, and half of that is still good. The best pieces I save for later, except for a beautiful ripe cantaloupe, which I cannot resist. As I reach for my pocket knife my mouth waters like the fountain in the big apartment complex and my hands tremble as they did when I first caressed Allie. Slowly, very slowly, I slice off a thin, narrow strip of peeling from pole to pole. The bouquet is breathtaking. I carve out one small bite for myself and one for Ben, who swallows his immediately. I, on the other hand, roll the morsel around and around with my tongue, then nibble gently until the fragment is mushy and the inside of my mouth is coated with a veneer of pulp. Never have I tasted anything so good.

I peel the entire melon as slowly as I can manage, taking care to lose as little of the fruit as possible. When the voluptuous yellow-orange orb is fully exposed, bright as the sun, I sink all my teeth into the soft flesh, pressing it hard against my tongue and palate. The next few moments are obscene, disgusting, paradisical. Ben watches the entire production closely, a long drool hanging suggestively from his fuzzy mouth.

While he works at an overripe banana I devour a nectarine, a bunch of grapes and, finally, a golden apple. The feast calls up a happy afternoon in chemistry lab, where our teacher passed around little bottles containing the essences of various fruits, some of which I had never heard of. They all smelled wonderful, but not as good as the aroma of the Korean grocery distilled into this beautiful basket, right, Ben? Mr. Brown thought I would become a scientist some day, Ben, but I told him I was going to be a poet and philosopher. We were both wrong, weren't we, my friend?

59

VINCENT

On Sundays, rain or shine, a painter comes to the park. From our usual bench we watch as he sets up his easel, mumbling all the while, *sotto voce*, about life's little tricks and absurdities. By the time he has dabbed some acrylic onto the canvas, already layered with excrescences of every possible hue, a crowd of eight or ten spectators has formed behind him. Unlike van Gogh he still has both his ears but only one arm, the missing one serving as an early topic of conversation among the ad hoc committee of judges.

All spring and summer he has worked at the same canvas, adding layer after layer of fast-drying pigment until it is so thick it resembles an upended mountain range. Sometimes he cries out as he slaps on more paint, other times he laughs like crazy Otto, who has joined the onlookers. Each layer is applied violently and without apparent reason. No one understands what he is up to, but no one can take his eyes off the work-in-progress. "It's a picture of hell," one critic opines. "No, it's a bad dream," argues another. Half the connoisseurs love it, the other half passionately hate it—there is no middle ground.

I think I know why, Ben. I think the painting represents nothing less than life itself, at once beautiful and ugly, purposeful and pointless, its roots buried deep in the past, yet constantly changing—one unpredictable, irreversible brushstroke after another.

After an hour of frenetic activity Vincent suddenly throws his palette and brushes into his case, slams it shut, grabs his unfinished masterpiece and strides off, still talking to himself. The onlookers, stunned, their lives under his arm, watch him go in profound silence.

When everyone has drifted away, crazy Otto, his blue knit hat splattered by a greenish-white pigeon dropping, stands right where he was, as he always does when Vincent leaves, a pair of shiny tears trickling down his huge round face.

60
BRIGITTE

We return to our sleeping place under a clear, bright sky. It has turned cooler again, and I happily anticipate a good, uninterrupted night's sleep. But, as my mother might have said, it was not meant to be.

It is Ben, of course, who finds her first. She is lying on top of our unfilled air mattress and army blanket, fully clothed and sound asleep. He sniffs; she returns a muffled sound. He nudges; she stirs. He whines, she jerks awake and bolts upright. Fortunately, she does not scream.

Ben, who will always be a puppy, rolls immediately onto his back, his legs spread obscenely. She takes the hint and scratches his belly. His eyes close in ecstasy. She looks up at me and smiles, too.

She is only twelve or thirteen and dressed in brand-new jeans whose knees are fashionably worn, like my own. Her matching suede jacket and shoes are equally stylish, as are the nose jewel and purple Mohawk. An expensive overnight bag completes the ensemble.

She sees that I am taking everything in and anticipates my unasked question. "I've run away," she explains. "Please don't try to send me back. I won't go, and it will spoil everything." Her voice sounds much like the young Judy Garland's in *The Wizard of Oz.*

"How can I send you back? I don't know where you live."

"I won't bother you. I'll sleep out here."

"We sleep out here, too."

"Oh—I thought...."

"I ran away also. So did Ben, maybe."

"Ben—that's a nice name."

"He's a nice dog."

"Where did he get that name?"

"It's my father's name."
"That's—like—pretty funny."
"What isn't?"

We all share a pretzel and a candy bar (Brigitte's contribution). While I blow up the air mattress she returns to the street to empty her bladder behind a bush for greater privacy. We talk late into the night.

Brigitte is smart, quite mature in many ways, yet very innocent, trusting. With her head resting on my chest she tells me everything. As I suspected, her parents have important careers. She never sees them. They don't have time for her, don't understand her, yet they won't let her *do* anything. When she can no longer stay awake I say goodnight and promise that we will talk again in the morning. But just before she falls asleep I make a terrible mistake: I tell her I would be happy to call her parents, who must be very worried about her disappearance. In the morning she is gone.

> Dear Brigitte,
>
> I'm sorry I disappointed you. I think we could have been friends. Even though I knew you for only a short time, I liked you a lot and miss you very much. I hope with all my heart that you are safe and happy now.
>
> Love, Ben and I

61

The Blind Man

The sky is a solid gray, without form, and void. There is no indication that behind the thick clouds shines a bright blue sky, a fiery yellow sun. It is cold, too, and damp: it's almost certainly going to rain. Ben, unconcerned about the meteorological conditions, dozes at my feet, dreaming, perhaps, of slow-moving squirrels. A child meanders close by, reaches down to touch him. His mother, frowning deeply, jerks her away. I want to tell the angular woman that neither Ben nor I has a communicable disease, but she wouldn't believe it, nor anything else we might say to her.

Toward us wends a man with a peculiar malady: he can't lift his head or shoulders. His spine and neck are frozen at a perfect ninety-degree angle, forcing him to focus forever on the piston-like movements of his wingtip shoes, about which he must know all that can be known. He seems fit enough, otherwise, and he strides briskly toward his unseen destination. Most of the scattered strollers step out of his way, but now and then two or three students, themselves blinded by the brilliance of their conversation, nearly crash into him before he stops and neatly whirls around them, like some kind of automated toy.

It starts to drizzle. Ben wakes up, yawns, watches the bent-over man pass a few yards away then grow smaller and smaller as he dances his fitful waltz down the damp gray walk, finally disappearing under the arch. Ben seems saddened by this spectacle until I remind him that almost everyone we see suffers from the same malady, able to focus his attention only as far as a footstep ahead, never knowing, nor much caring, what crevices or cliffs lie a little farther down the winding path.

The rain smells good. "Let's go see if the pretzel man has any stale bites to throw away," I suggest. Ben is up immediately, jerking me toward the little outdoor kitchen at the corner of the park, his mouth already drooling hopefully.

62

MUSIC

Near the children's corner a solitary flute player runs through a series of arpeggios before breaking into a mournful air. Ben, who has been sleeping at my feet, pricks up his ears to listen. When the sad refrain suddenly segues into a lively minuet he swings his massive head to gaze at me with one eye, wondering, I suspect, if I would care to dance.

The trees, too, are filled with flutists, young robins and sparrows practicing their lively tunes from their newly-discovered songbooks. They are joined by the squirrels, who, caught up in the general celebration, screech their terrible harmonies. The dogs in the run get into the act, their barks and howls the woodwinds of this large urban orchestra, whose chorus is provided by the chatter of the endlessly passing faculty and students and, of course, by the shouting and babble of the always energetic children in the playground. And everywhere the pigeons bob their heads in time to the plangent music.

Outside the park the horns of the trucks and taxis make their brassy contributions, and a nearby jackhammer supplies ample percussion. A wailing fire truck gives the piece a distinctly modern touch, and Ben, tired of being a wallflower, jumps up to perform his graceful pirouettes.

The symphony, though discordant, is soothing: it is the sound of life. As I am about to doze off I am startled to hear a pure, crystalline voice rise above the blaring background. It is too much for Mabel, whose arms are raised to the sky in heavenly praise. Ben immediately tugs me in her direction.

I only wish I could ask her what she finds so moving in the performance. She, who comprehends little else, seems to understand the complex polyphony of the park. Perhaps she alone has caught a glimpse of the score, and is following the baton of its invisible Conductor.

63

The Pretzel Man

From the door of the savings and loan we sometimes see the pretzel man pushing his heavy cart up the street on his way to the park, smiling and hopeful. Later, we find him standing across from the library shouting at the students as they come out for a break: "Hot pretzels—softer than a baby's bottom!" Whether business has been good or bad we can always count on him for a stale one, or one that has fallen to the ground some time before we arrive, though it is often still warm, still baby-bottom soft. He explains that he had a dog like Ben once—a transparent attempt to justify his extraordinary generosity. But Mabel and Otto and some of the other regulars also realize a handout from time to time, and none of them has a canine companion, discounting those no one else can see.

The pretzel man is not very busy this breezy, late September afternoon, and when Ben pulls me over to his stand I ask him how he got into the fast-food business. While he searches for a free sample he literally sings his recent history, a kind of urban chantey recounting his life as service station attendant, short-order cook, chauffeur, door-to-door salesman, school photographer, gardener. All of this while waiting for someone to buy his first novel, a story about a service station attendant who becomes a short-order cook who becomes a chauffeur, etc., etc. Everyone he has ever met is in there, including Ben and me, who are, in fact, making an appearance in the current paragraph, and the novel grows and grows. The ending, however, never varies: he meets a beautiful, pretzel-loving girl whose father is president of a conglomerate that owns several large publishing companies. His manuscript, which has been rejected by every editor in the country, becomes a bestseller, he marries the girl, and they live happily ever after.

A big man and strong, he laughs heartily at the end of his tale, but it is not the giggle of a crazy Otto, nor the bitter shriek of the Korean grocer. It is the helpless chuckle of a man who realizes he is wasting his life in search of a pipe dream, a pursuit over which he, nonetheless, has no control. I, who have also made the hopeless cause into a vocation, laugh too.

He hands Ben and me a perfect specimen, which, he claims, he retrieved from the ground earlier. And perhaps he did, though it is still clean and fresh. But it is he, the pretzel man, who is warm, and soft as a baby's bottom.

64

STATUES

On the main sidewalk of the park, overlooking the central arena, stands Garibaldi, long ago blinded by the sun. He is a favorite resting place for the pigeons because he never moves, never startles them into panicky flight like the people hurrying by not far below. Pockmarked by wind-tossed sand and acid rains, he has been graffitied, hatted, spray-painted, garlanded, and diapered by any number of fraternity freshmen. But, while most of the perpetrators have disappeared from the scene over the decades, he stands forever facing the golden sunsets, perpetually unperturbed.

Against a trash can to his right leans a wooden box, the kind favored by fruit packers. On a whim I drag the empty crate to a grassy area of the park, step onto my makeshift pedestal and gaze stoically toward the east.

Ben, who is quicker on the uptake than most people, lies down facing the same direction, the hint of a silly grin on his face.

In a few minutes we get our first double-take; a man bangs to a stop, his briefcase swinging out in front of him in businesslike testament to Newton's law of inertia. He stares, scrutinizes the box for a name, shrugs and moves on.

Ten minutes later a pair of women carrying heavy shopping bags pause to stare at us and rest their feet.

"What is it—a monument to the homeless or somethin'?"

"I don't know, Pearl, but the guy that carved it can do my turkey any time."

"All except for the dog. There ain't no dog like that nowhere."

They pick up their parcels and waddle on, engaged in tired conversation about dinner and family.

Drunk with success, we wait for yet another audience. Several more people pass by—a man yelling at his female companion; a gaggle of skateboarders; a drunk combing his hair with a fork. None of them takes notice. Finally, a cocky pre-adolescent, chomping hard on a huge wad of bubble gum, spots us. Without hesitation he picks up a stone and lets fly right at my crotch. Instinctively my hands rush down to block the shot. His mouth falls open, exposing the rubbery pink gum.

"Go away, kid."

He runs back to his mother, who has seen him throw something at the monument to homelessness. She boxes his ears and hustles the screeching youth out of the park.

Ben, I think I know why some people become actors!

65

Grass

Whenever we pass by the big churches lining the broad avenue leading to the park Ben always thrusts his snout between the bars of the tall iron fences for deep whiffs of the rich, green grass and the manicured flower gardens beyond. It must seem odd to him that no one has marked these virgin fields with pungent and unique scents, as if such venerable grounds are above the vulgarities and profanities of life. Perhaps in heaven there are no dogs, my friend, or, if there are, they do not urinate. Would you like to go to a place like that?

As for me the beautiful grass, like so many things, takes me home to the big front yard where I used to run, barefooted and fast, after baseballs and frisbees thrown by my father, my mother fretting that I would get too near the road. How good that prickly lawn felt, how I would love to see and feel it again! Real grass, Ben, with no iron bars around it!

Along one of these fences paces a man peddling another kind of grass: for a few dollars we could have a good smoke. Ben lopes ahead toward the skinny guy, who freaks out. "Jesus Christ," he pleads, "get him away from me." A vain prayer, but sincere, unlike many of those offered on peaceful Sunday mornings inside the stony edifice behind the blackened barricade. When his Savior does not respond he shrieks and dashes across the street, nearly meeting his Maker on the fender of a speeding limousine.

An idea strikes me, but none of the church officials is around to tell it to: why not sell walks on the grass for dogs at, say, 25¢ a minute? Another quarter for a piss, fifty cents a crap? The lawn would no longer resemble the perfect terraces of heaven, but perhaps it would remind the flock that their cathedral is still firmly rooted in the sweet-smelling earth, with all its worldly problems, that the road to salvation is paved not with pretty flowers but with excrement. As a bonus, the money could be used to help solve some of those earthly concerns, rather than send another missionary to save the souls of people who are dying of starvation and disease all over this desperate planet....

C'mon, Ben. No one is listening.

66
Dead Tree

Along the street in front of the movie theater stands a row of young elm trees planted on a drizzly day last spring, remember, Ben? Most of them are thriving, their yellow-green leaves bright in the dazzling sunshine, but, for some reason, one has become ill and is dying, like a feverish child. It seems odd, but the demise of a tree is almost as moving as the death of a personal acquaintance, and doubly distressing when the lifeless corpse is left standing, its naked limbs outstretched, pleading for salvation. An ancient, gnarled oak tree stimulates much the same affection we feel for an old, arthritic grandfather. Both have lived long lives, have seen the world through the best and the worst of its history, and we are equally saddened by their respective passing. But it's even more tragic when the tree is a sapling, whose death throes generate much the same emotions as do those of a child.

Do you suppose they have feelings, Ben? A few days before last year's end, before I knew you, my friend, I came across the place where they sell Christmas trees. All the ones nobody wanted were lying in the blowing snow, their lives having been cut short for nothing. I stood each of them up and decorated it with a piece of red ribbon I had found. It may be hard to believe, but every one of those trees smelled twice as good after its little bangle was in place, and I could swear their drooping branches lifted a little.

A dying tree doesn't know it is doomed, but we do, and it gets us every time.

67
Twins

Look, Ben—here come the twins! Two strikingly attractive co-eds, dressed exactly alike except for the dissident colors of their sweatpants, approach with slow, feminine strides, as majestic as a pair of giraffes. Their long blond hair, their noses and mouths, their expressions and experiences are identical. We have seen them before, always lockstepped in each other's silent company, as if mortally afraid of separation, Siamese twins joined at the psyche. I wonder, as we watch them march to their secret, inner rhythm, whether they have, or ever have had, independent thoughts, personal feelings. They are beautiful but somehow sad, a tragic alliance.

Two male students, coming the other way, turn to stare and offer flattering comments, which the girls, in their unspoken conspiracy, ignore. A few other passersby take note of the remarkable phenomenon; most hurry along to their endless pursuits without noticing the twins, or anything. A child who has not yet learned not to see, points and shouts: "Mommy! There are two of her!" But nothing fazes them, not even the near demise of a black squirrel, who runs across the path of an oncoming taxi and into the park. On the other hand Ben, who is constantly fazed, makes a sudden lurch toward Blackie; it is all I can do to hold him back. The girls proceed down the sidewalk, their flawless gait as charming and mysterious as life itself.

Why do you suppose they always wear those sweat pants, Ben—one blue, the other green: to tell themselves apart? Would you like to have an identical twin, my friend? Would you be satisfied with half a life? Look around you at all the people hurrying by, all identical to each other, all terrified of being different from everyone else, of expressing anything afield: would you like to be one of them? A tuplet? Would you trade your life for one of their empty souls?

Ben, who has no interest in sociology, waits impatiently for an oatmeal raisin cookie.

68

STREET FAIR

Ben tugs me toward the sharp, strong aromas of sizzling sausages and fresh-spun cotton candy and I do not resist, for these are not the essences of seared meat and burnt sugar, but of blithesome youth.

Poor as we were, Mom always made sure I had a little money for the fair. Although there wasn't enough for many rides or shows, the wonderful smells alone were worth the price of admission, even without the noise, the excitement, the kaleidoscopic colors, especially after dark when the sky was bright with the white, yellow, and green lights of the buzz bomber, the merry-go-round, the caterpillar, and my favorite, the tilt-a-whirl!

What could be more awesome than the mile-high Ferris wheel? More beautiful than the majestic trotting horses, their manes flying, who seemed to give everything they had to their silky drivers? More darkly fascinating than the unfortunates with their large, sad eyes, on display in the seedy side shows? More satisfying than a good bash with a bumper car? More redolent than the hay in the animal barns?

Ben prefers to focus on the present. His eyes are on a table filled with happy people dining alfresco. One of the group, holding his plate away from a foul-smelling panhandler, bellows, "Get out of here, you bum!"

The beggar, whose shoulder-length hair is even longer and stringier than my own, marches off in mock dismay. "Please—I have a Ph.D. Call me *Dr.* Bum!" The diner's female companion, amused, flings the ex-professor a quarter.

I couldn't wait to take Chris to the fair the first time, Ben! How he loved the little red and blue cars, the wooden horses of the carousel, the twirly soft ice cream cones. And how careful I was to make sure he didn't get lost, like I did from my mother when I was his age. I will never forget the hug I got when she found me, my hungry friend!

Ben's close scrutiny is rewarded by a dropped sandwich, which disappears in two bites. His obsession satisfied, he is content to accompany me to the rides, where all the kids have congregated. Along the way we pass the games of chance—the unbreakable balloons, the unmovable cement milk bottles—with their wiry hawkers and wary clientele. *Plus ça change....*

Look, Ben, look at all the children in the little cars! Around and around they go, bemusedly whirling their steering wheels to no avail. A little boy looks hard for his mother's eyes, finally finds them. He beams: I love you, Mom! I love you!

69

THE JUGGLER

It must be Sunday: the children in the playground are supervised by their parents, rather than people of other races, creeds, colors, or national origins. We watch in delight as they swarm all over the monkey pole, yelling and jabbering about whatever comes into their little heads, practicing for adulthood. A sign posted on the great red oak tree announces that rat poison is everywhere. "Don't eat anything, Ben!"

In the central arena a student-cum-juggler is balancing a football on his forehead. All around him lie the rest of his trappings: tennis balls, bowling pins, unlit torches, unsheathed swords. Comics, acrobats and other entertainers frequent this stage, but his is a new face, one we have not seen before. An expectant crowd has already gathered and is waiting patiently for the promised excitement. From the chess tables: "Bang!" A few heads turn.

Unlike the other jugglers we have seen in the park he delivers no patter, no visual or verbal humor—he simply proceeds. Three tennis balls fly. He drops them. His audience, unsure of how to respond, remains silent. The student retrieves the balls, begins again. When he drops them a second time the crowd, on firmer ground, starts to titter: it is obviously a comic routine. Crazy Otto, taking his cue from the others, laughs heartily. Everyone seems curiously relieved. Then he gets it right and the crowd, still smiling, applauds politely, as does Otto, only louder.

"Bang!"

The next part of the act also goes smoothly, even when the bowling pins go through the legs and around the back. It is only when the sweating student tries it from the seat of his unicycle that everything goes haywire: one of the pins actually lands on his head with a thunk. The people wince and make uncomfortable noises.

The tension mounts as he picks up the torches and lights them with a whoosh. Again, all is well until the end. A gasp from the crowd—the juggler's hair has caught fire! He beats it out with his fists. It is not a comedy routine at all, but the maiden performance of an amateur.

"Bang!"

Dripping with perspiration he puts out the torches and grimly picks up the swords. Someone yells, "NO!" But he ignores her and all of us, and the blades go flying. For a long moment no one breathes: it is not a trio of sabers we see gleaming in the garish sun, but our own cut and bleeding hearts.

70

THE ELEPHANT MAN

Sometimes, on bright yellow mornings, we come across the man whose feet are covered by a crusty fungus, asleep against the fence of the big apartment complex. Despite the fetor, Ben invariably tugs me close for a good whiff of his decaying body, which may not have known soap or water for years. I always pull him across the street, but not before he has filled his lungs with the rich effluvium.

This day is different. When we get within half a block of the supine figure, it is Ben who wants to visit the opposite curb. Realizing that something must be wrong I wrap his rope around a light pole and circle to approach the prone figure from upwind.

He appears to be sleeping soundly as usual, but when I inch closer I can see that his eyes and mouth are open, his chest still, his face puffy and gray. Sometime during the night, not far from our subterranean home, he must have simply lay down and died. Perhaps he rotted to death.

As I hurry back to retrieve my companion the icy fingers of sorrow grip my soul—the elephant man is dead! Someone whose life touched our own, and thus became a part of it, is gone. But it is much more than that. It's not just the death of a neighbor to whom I have never spoken that tears at the fabric of my being, nor even the stark realization that this might well have been my father. I have caught a glimpse of the future, a preview of my own demise, possibly under similar circumstances, and someone who is now Chris's age is bending over me, afraid to touch my stinking body.

I return, trembling, to my companion, whose snout is in close, zig-zag pursuit of a large black ant; he has already forgotten the elephant man.

C'mon, Ben, let's go find a policeman.

71

LEADER OF THE PACK

Preoccupied by myriad thoughts on a host of topics I pay no attention to the traffic until Ben forcefully stops me from stumbling into the path of an oncoming taxi whose horn, evidently, is malfunctional, like myself. The driver screeches to a halt, curses half-heartedly at me, nervously lights a cigarette. I shrug at him and move on. Ben takes the lead again and prances a trifle more jauntily than usual the rest of the way to the park.

In the run he is more the wise, helpful uncle, less the clown. Only when Fricka shows up does he become his foolish self, bowling her over at the gate and allowing her to chew on his bent ear before they are off to a roaring game of nip-the-throat. When I tell Sung Tieng what he did earlier she becomes excited. "It is good sign," she pronounces. "This your lucky day!"

At the savings and loan I half expect someone to drop a $100 bill into my cup, but our fortune is actually below average: our efforts bring in barely enough for food, with nothing to add to our meager savings. We move on to the Korean grocery and deli a little later than usual, Ben as excited as if we were going to the most fascinating place in the city, and perhaps it is.

Inside, I remember Ben's heroic deed and decide to reward him with one of the expensive chew sticks I have seen hanging on the back wall on previous visits. But when I pull my wallet from my hip pocket a teenager grabs it roughly from my hands and tears out of the store.

"Hey!"

The little money is unimportant, but the pictures of Allie and Chris are the only mementos I have of our time together. Ben, as if long expecting something like this to happen, somehow pulls himself free of the hydrant and gives chase. Halfway down the block he bowls the kid over and my billfold goes flying. Ignoring the thief, Ben retrieves it and lopes easily back to me with the prize hanging from his mouth like a pigeon or squirrel caught napping, at last.

Aware now that he can get loose whenever he wants, I nonetheless loop his rope back around the fireplug and finish the transaction, to much joking and laughter from the owner, knowing that Ben can leave at will, but knowing also that he won't budge unless circumstances demand it. And I know something else, too: though he has been pretending otherwise all along, it is Ben who is the leader of our pack.

72

Blue Sky

What a beautiful day, Ben. I have never seen the sky so blue or so clear, even when I was a boy. It's as if it were a large robin's egg and the entire world an embryo waiting to be born. I bet the dogs in the run will be extremely frisky today, as you were when you brought me your newspaper before I was even awake—shall we go see?

How fresh and clean the sidewalk seems! Did someone wash it, do you suppose? See how the iron fence against which the elephant man died reflects the vibrant rays of the sun! What's this—did someone paint the fire hydrants and trash cans yesterday? Everything seems different today, all the layers of dirt and despair have been stripped away by last night's rain and the intense laser light of morning.

I remember another day like this: Allie's brother took me for a ride in his rented airplane. You should see what the Earth looks like from a mile up on a supremely clear day, my friend, green and placid like the lawn around the big church on the corner; then you would know what the lucky birds know. It is even better from outer space, they say, so wonderful that even hardened astronauts have been known to weep at the sight of its aquamarine splendor. The pictures I have seen of our planet remind me of a beautiful glass marble I won from my friend Jack when I was a boy. It was the cerulean blue of the sky on a day like this one, with wisps of white embedded inside like slow-moving clouds.

How I loved that perfect shooter, which was more precious than any gem to me.

But you and I don't have to fly high to find beauty, do we, my friend—not as long as we can come to the park on a day like this. Look at the smile on Mabel's pretty face! And there's the man with no feet, keeping time to a silent song with one of his aluminum crutches, which shines like a silver baton. Even Crazy Otto seems quite contented, over there by the playground, listening to the children, who chirp like birds, and the birds, chattering like children. How happy the dogs are, Ben—just like you!

Here come Fricka and Daisy! Wait ... Wait ... let me open the gate for you!

73

Peace

Every Sunday a tall, elderly woman wearing a sandwich board comes to the park. Her wants are few and simple: WE SEEK A WORLD FREE OF NUCLEAR WAR .... For hours she stands silently, alone. No one stops to discuss the matter with her, no car honks in support. Her bearing is regal, her quiet calmness noble. Perhaps the "WE" is royal.

Ben and I, on our way back from the deli with our lunch, pause across the street to watch her, and I imagine for a moment that we live in the kind of world she longs for, one without intolerance and fear. In my nonexistent universe the peace lady arrives with her board, but she is not alone for long. A man barreling by stops without a word, sets down his bulging briefcase, and takes his place beside her. A second later a bright-eyed co-ed joins them, followed in rapid order by a construction worker, a cop, a mother and her two children. Others join the group until the sidewalk is crowded with people, and the street with honking vehicles. Soon the whole park is crammed with supporters, some waving their own signs, others singing and chanting: PEACE! PEACE! The crowd grows and grows until everyone in the city has come to join this glorious movement. Someone starts to play a flute, others begin to dance, and children with flowers in their hair—

Ben, who wants to eat, tugs at his rope. I open my eyes. Across the street stands the peace lady, as always. But she is not alone. With her is crazy Otto, rigid as Garibaldi, the two of them the vanguard of a new society. Behind them a bum roots around in a trash receptacle, searching for cigarette butts, a hamburger carton, a beer can, a life.

74

Leaves

An advertisement posted on the bulletin board near the rest rooms announces the upcoming Oktoberfest at the student union. All the beer you can drink—shall we go, Ben?

To me, the very word "October" evokes the pleasant aroma of smoldering leaves—the ones Dad used to stack in tall piles for me to jump into before he burned them. What a wonderful smell they had, as did the sweet smoke that rose from them like spirits seeking a leafy heaven. Is this your favorite time of year also, my friend, when the foliage drips from the trees like liquid gold, and the still air is redolent of raked earth? Don't you wish every month could be as colorful and fragrant as this one?

Allie once told me she hated autumn, would you believe it? She saw it as the season of death and decay! I could never convince her that even as the withered leaves of the sun-drenched oaks and maples fell to the earth, from which they came, next year's new green growth was already coming to life in its twiggy womb. Autumn is a time of renewal and regeneration for which verdant spring unfairly gets all the credit.

On the other hand, the beautiful fall foliage is not autumn's doing, as you might suppose, but the undiscovered talent of spring's magical artistry. The brilliant reds and yellows have been there all along; they were simply overwhelmed by the thicker veil of summer's green facade. I bet even you were fooled, my perceptive friend, though colors are not your forte.

But we should not judge this chicanery too harshly. Don't we all put on disguises from time to time to conceal our true colors, even from those we love? Indeed, are we always truthful with ourselves? If we could only strip away our phony veneer, what beautiful hues we might find underneath!

75

BOOKS

On the sidewalk in front of the library someone has set up a used-book stall. Here one can find the great literary figures of the world, and works on every topic under the golden sun, all for the princely sum of 50 cents for hardcovers (5/$2), a quarter for paperbacks (5/$1). A ring of frugal browsers is quickly drawn in, like so many iron filings, jostling for position, loathe to give way to the milling usurpers behind them.

A panhandler wearing a signboard with interchangeable slats works the crowd, those waiting for a place at the table. When UNEMPLOYED EXECUTIVE generates no response he shifts to BEHIND IN ALIMONY PAYMENTS. A few sympathetic quarters tinkle into his cup.

The books themselves are faded, lusterless, having lost their bright, colorful jackets long ago. They remind me of pressed flowers, Ben, whose splendor and vitality are diminished with time, yet whose inherent beauty is undimmed in memory.

A car chugs by, its windows open, its radio at full volume.... BOOM ... BOOM ... BOOM ... BOOM .... An elderly woman is chasing it—"MORRIS!" she wails in a feeble voice. "MY KEYS! MORRIS!!!" The kid pulls away, his head bobbing to the beat of the drums.

How well I remember my first book, Ben—you would have loved it too. It was *The Swiss Family Robinson,* a story about a family shipwrecked on an uninhabited island, unspoiled by noise and pollution, undamaged by progress. I dreamed about that book, constructed worlds of my own, pretended to be their king. I hope Chris has found that wonderful volume among the artifacts of my childhood.

If I had one of those nice apartments between here and the river, my friend, I would line its walls with books, and sit among the dusty leaves inhaling their bouquet as you would a sign pole or fire hydrant, drawing into my soul the wisdom and beauty of the world, the pressed flowers of the mind.

76

FILMMAKING

At the dog run Sung Tieng invites Ben and me for dinner on Sunday. I decline, not because I do not like her—I would enjoy meeting her husband, the biochemist, and their two clever children—but because I have no way to repay the compliment. She is disappointed, though I think she understands, and we watch as Ben and Fricka play keepaway with the rubber newspaper until she has to leave for work.

Near the playground a film crew has set the stage for Scene 18, Take 1, of a movie whose title I never learned. A young woman (one of the technicians tells me, as he scratches Ben's head with one hand and his own with the other) is supposed to run across the grass in the rain to meet her lover right in front of the main camera, only she slips and falls instead. There is little turf in this section of the park, and the sky is only partly cloudy, but no matter—they will create fake grass, produce artificial rain and, unbelievably, bogus sunlight as well.

Nothing happens for the next forty-five minutes. The crew members chit and chat, drink coffee, munch donuts, drink more coffee. The disappointed onlookers drift away and we, too, must take our leave. Reluctantly, for there is something magical about the movie business, with its unrepressed theatrics and glamour.

We leave the savings and loan a little earlier than usual and return to the park to enjoy the filmmaking, along with our lunch, only to discover that Scene 18 is not yet in the can. There are lights and camera, but no action. The film crew is still drinking coffee, still yakking among themselves.

A half-hour passes. At last, from a huge trailer fed by countless umbilicals, a tiny figure in a vivid blue slicker emerges. She is beautiful, her features chisel-perfect. Yet she seems fragile, unreal, a brightly-colored wraith. She takes a seat on a folding chair and, with everyone else, awaits final lighting adjustments. No one in the small crowd can take his eyes off her. Otto shows up, laughs, moves on.

Ben—everything is ready! The grass mat is swept and straightened, both sun and rain come on. The girl is led to her mark. The striped board snaps (just like in the movies!), the girl starts running. After a few steps she tumbles unconvincingly onto the wet, green carpet, looks up, wipes the rain and tears dramatically from her eyes, picks herself up and staggers on.

"Cut! Let's try it again...."

The wet blue starlet is led back to her trailer. The weather is turned off, the cameras pull back, the technicians begin to prepare for another take. The crowd disperses again.

Shall I tell you what I would do if I had a camera, Ben? I would set it up right here, turn it on, and film everything that happens in the park, with real clouds and real people and unrehearsed joy and sorrow.

But who would want to see it?

77

THE POET

Ragged and gaunt, a man we have not seen before stands, statuesquely, beside his little cardboard table, on which is propped a dirty, handwritten sign: POEMS $.25. For very little remuneration he will create an ode for any occasion, idea, or subject. Though he appears to be on the threshold of death, a barely-clothed skeleton, his eyes are as bright as the stars. It is difficult to tell whether their terrible fire is born of out fever or desperation, fathered, perhaps, by hunger or illness. But what is he doing here by the river, rather than on some busy street corner?

BEN AND I

I have a quarter, Ben—let's buy a poem! As excited by this extravagant prospect as am I, my eager companion trots over to the bard and plunges his snout into the old man's crotch—he has never learned subtlety in the matter of satisfying his insatiable curiosity. The poet doesn't flinch, or even blink, though he doesn't seem to be blind.

I place the coin in his grimy hand. It clatters against the fleshless bone. The digits quickly close, the man comes to life. "What is the subject?" he demands, in a thick raspy voice coated with phlegm and despair.

"Ben," I respond. "A beautiful poem about my friend here."

The obsidian eyes stare intently into the one of Ben's that returns their gaze. The greasy hair adds an unnecessary burden to the brittle ankles and tiny feet, sandal-clad despite the chill in the air. I begin to wonder whether we are a single moment too late, whether the poet is about to collapse like an old house riddled with termites, leaving a tiny pile of dust covered by a few old rags.

But no: with what seems to be his last ounce of strength he finesses a scrap of paper from the box, scribbles "BEN" at the top of the preprinted opus and hands it to me, thereby concluding our transaction. He immediately resumes his former position, where he will remain, presumably, until the clank of another coin in his skeletal palm reawakens him, like some antiquated arcade contraption. Afraid that any hint of a negative reaction would prove disastrous, I lead Ben to the other side of the pier, where I read the poem to him.

BEN

I pulled three quarters from my jeans
And plunked them down beside the icy glass.
C'mon, turkey, it's a buck, she said,
And wiped her fingers on a striped towel.
I said, Oh, I didn't know—
That's all I have today.
She pulled her tiny nose,
Eyed me sideways, and
Taking back the drink,
Began to pour it out.
Whoa! I said. What do we gain
By dribbling it away?
You could dump out half
And take four of my bits;

> Or a fourth, and you can have all six.
> She kept that hardened look
> But drained away the upper part,
> Pushed it back to me and
> Slid the money wetly to her other hand.
> Then she turned and walked away.
> I wanted to say a word to get her back—
> Something to make her think
> That I was not a piece of shit.
> Not out, but just a little down . . . .
> If I ever get a bill together, why,
> I'm coming back to this place!

Well, Ben, I suppose you're in there between the lines somewhere, as are we all.

78

THE CHILDREN

Ben and I like to watch the little school children as they pass through the park on their way to some high adventure, all strung together like a pearl necklace in bright yellow vests. We see them giggling their way across the street in perfect innocence, never looking to the right or left but trusting their precious lives to their teachers, one at the head of the sinuous organism, the other bringing up the rear.

Here they come, Ben—look at them smile! He peers at them with one eye; the other continues to scrutinize a nearby squirrel. Two by two they approach us, each holding the hand of a partner, all talking at once. Who knows what tremendous visions race through their untroubled minds—fine lunches; championship games of jacks; clean, cool sheets; great puddles they have known? I try hard to remember the thoughts that filled my head all those years ago, but nothing comes forth except the first day of school, Mom waving good-bye, an enormous vat of wonderful-smelling paste waiting in the windowsill.

The approaching children finally see Ben; they veer toward him, as do all children when he comes into view. The whole line curves over like a great banana to offer tiny fingers to smell. "Don't touch him!" the hind teacher orders. "He might bite!" It is not clear whether she means Ben or myself, but in this way the youth of another generation learn to fear every animal they might encounter, or any bearded man in a tattered coat, for the rest of their lives.

But two or three of the group don't believe the propaganda. They strain hard to get closer until the chaperone in front straightens the line with a firm tug. Ben wags his tail hopefully, but the children are all drawn away. The adventuresome few glance back wistfully; the rest chatter away as if someone were listening, and never notice Ben's disappointment, nor the flaming reds and golds of the oak and elm trees.

If I had any money, Ben, I would put it on those few kids who refused to be intimidated even when they were so instructed. If the world somehow manages to survive itself, it will be because of the tenacious courage of a few brave souls like them.

79

DUKE

Whenever Duke, the German shepherd, comes to the dog run I try to keep Ben away from his human companion. Too many times I have seen the dog snap or snarl at anyone who gets close to this man, who thinks such episodes hilarious. It's not Duke's fault, he is not a bad dog—there are very few bad dogs—he has simply been trained too well.

Over the past several months I have come to believe there are very few bad people, either, only those who have become alienated through circumstances beyond their control. Yet, there are just as many who go out of their way to help others without expecting reward or recognition. A few days ago we watched a policeman climb a cherry tree to retrieve a stray kitten who had been living under a dumpster near one of the girls' dormitories. After he had coaxed it into his outstretched hand he fell out of the tree, injuring his leg and back, but he never let go of his prize.

The cop hobbled away with the scrawny little thing clutched tightly to his chest.

My journal is filled with incidents like that. Consider this: a couple of months ago I saw a well-dressed man stuff a $20 bill under a sleeping drunk, who, but for the grace of God, might have been himself. And there's the pigeon man, and the old woman who brings unshelled peanuts for the squirrels every day, rain or shine. The retired banker who picks up trash and debris in and around the park, making up for all the years he neglected it and, I suppose, the world in general. Taxi drivers who screech to a halt and give directions to people who are puzzling over a map. I vividly remember a ragged bum who somehow procured a sandwich and brought it back to another man in even worse shape than himself. And of course there are all the people who, as they exit the savings and loan, give us money for no reason other than goodness of heart.

I think that's why our species is so interesting, Ben. Individually we are fundamentally good. The mystery is why we, as a group, a nation, a civilization, tend to wreak such mischief on each other and on the Earth itself. If we could learn to understand and resolve this dichotomy perhaps we could transform the world, for perhaps the first time since man appeared on the scene, to the paradise it might have been.

But you think it's the Garden of Eden already, don't you, my furry friend?

80

HALLOWEEN

Someone has left a clean, hardly torn sheet in the trash can near the playground and, for tonight, Ben becomes his own ghost. A born actor, he plays the role to the hilt. Although barely encumbered by his bulky costume he treads silently, stiff-legged, a dog from the grave.

Thus, beneath an enormous butterscotch moon we haunt the streets in the company of various ghouls and werewolves, each trying hard to frighten the others, but without much success: everyone knows these are phony fears, meant to inure the young against the real thing. Accordingly, there is also much hollow laughter.

BEN AND I

It was exactly a year ago that I saw Chris for the last time. He was dressed as a Klingon, one of the terrible, warmongering enemies of the starship Enterprise. Despite his near-invincibility, however, I could feel him pressing against my side as we made our Halloween rounds, afraid, I thought, that something unspeakable would leap out at him from behind a bush or tree. How I loved him that night, how I tried to allay his fears, while attempting to conceal my own. By the time we got home he was crying. But it had nothing to do with spooks and goblins; he had deduced somehow that I was leaving the next morning.

Ben moans and wails at every passing witch and vampire, and is rewarded with a few small confections. Some of these diminutive monsters feign terror at my own mask and costume, which I wear every day—it appears that the desire to be a comedian comes early. One or two of these anonymous clowns throw trash at us after passing because we have added nothing to their bulging packs, having nothing to give.

But generally the mood is light, the evening whimsical. It is only later, when they get older, that the brave children we have encountered will begin to understand that the terrors they have faced this night are real, that no amount of candy or phony merriment will drive them away.

81

Winter Chill

Want some breakfast, my friend?

I had a funny dream last night, Ben. I dreamed that Otto was a helium-filled balloon. When he laughed—you know his crazy laugh—he rose from the ground. I tried to grab him but I missed and he just floated away. Where do you suppose he was going?

Although the sun is shining brightly there is a chill in the air, the first sign of harsh winter. Ben, who is happy at any temperature, exhausts everyone in the dog run. Afterwards, at the savings and loan, he sleeps soundly, like a puppy, in the golden sunlight.

Lunch in the park is a memorable cup of pea soup from the Korean deli, with pita bread and strong green tea. The soup calls up an image of my mother, who always insisted I have a hot lunch, even on the warmest days. Ben settles for a hunk of the bread and his usual cookie before dozing off again while I, warmed by the steaming liquids, settle down to assimilate life as it groans and roars everywhere around us.

Around mid-afternoon a young man—probably a student—staggers by, pausing every few feet to weave for a moment or two, eyes glazed, before stumbling on, high as the sky on one or another drug. A few minutes later a dachshund wearing a bell on her collar prances by carrying a bag of donuts in her jaws, her mettle being tested by her guardian, perhaps. Ben opens one eye as she tinkles by, closes it again. From behind us comes a woman cradling something in her arms and singing softly to it. When she gets closer I see it is a cat, but whether it is dead or merely sleeping, I cannot tell. Vincent hurls one last blob of crimson onto his masterpiece and packs up, leaving a small group of onlookers to scratch and mutter. On the street a stretch limousine stops at the curb. The chauffeur jumps out, pulls a newspaper from an overflowing trash bin, climbs back in. The long black car speeds away.

It is nearly suppertime when we finally spot Otto, at about the time he usually departs, hanging around the playground sobbing and wringing his hands. Despite the cold he is without his peacoat. Ben begs me to let him go over. I acquiesce, but Otto pays no attention to him. Nor will he accept anything to eat. For nearly an hour he paces, seemingly at a loss, unable to sit or stand still for a second.

Long after nightfall a well-dressed couple show up. The man stands gazing at the deserted playground while the woman comes over to retrieve Otto. She is thirtyish, red-headed, attractive. Gently she persuades him to put on his coat and go with them, and they amble off in the direction of the arch. A sudden icy gust causes my teeth to chatter involuntarily.

Ben, who has followed them to the edge of the park, returns to me without enthusiasm, his breath rising languorously from his steaming nostrils.

82

BLACKIE

While I watch a sparrow preen itself in the branch above, Ben checks the base of a sycamore for evidence of trespass. On a bench to our left sits a middle-aged man drinking from a paper bag, fortifying himself for the day's vicissitudes. A cream-colored pigeon picks at his feet. The imbiber kicks at it and misses.

On the other side of the street Blackie, the squirrel, waits for an opportunity to cross. Undecided, he stands motionless except for his swishing tail, his worried eyes focused less on the oncoming traffic than on Ben, who hasn't yet noticed him. Finally, just as a taxi careens around the corner, he darts fitfully onto the pavement. Seeing what is about to happen, I freeze. So does Blackie. Though the cab is moving fast it takes forever to pass over him. Death, the ultimate black hole, slows time to a crawl.

Having expected the worst, I am relieved to find Blackie sitting in the middle of the street, apparently unharmed. He jumps up, scurries toward us, slips under the low fence. Once in the park, however, he begins a series of back flips, distracting Ben from his sentry duties. Unable to believe his eye, Ben stalks the injured animal. I yell at him, afraid he will tear Blackie apart before I can stop him. Deafened by his inbred urges he ignores my entreaty. Fickle time now speeds up. In an instant Ben is at the squirrel and has him in his mouth. "Ben! Drop him!" I scream, though I have never taught him this or any other command, and my plea falls on Ben's temporarily deaf ears. But instead of running off with his prize he turns around and trots briskly toward me, the limp animal dangling from his massive jaws like a rubber newspaper, and drops him at my feet.

I have no idea how badly Blackie is hurt, but he is no longer doing back flips. Ben sits, one eye on me, the other on the squirrel. I pick him up and cradle him in my arms. Though he weighs almost nothing, his rough coat pulses with life. His eyes burn as brightly as did those of the poet we met along the river not so long ago.

I decide to take him to the vet who treated Ben's gastrointestinal problem in May. But the office won't be open for at least another hour. I carry him to the bench still occupied by the man drinking from the paper bag, and gently lay him on the ground. Blackie sits up and looks around slowly, but otherwise doesn't move. Ben stands guard, glancing left and right and left again.

Suddenly, as if awakening from a bad dream, the squirrel whirls around and faces Ben for a moment before bolting to the nearest tree. Ben pretends to give chase. The squirrel easily beats him to the sycamore and runs all the way to the top before stopping. Ben sniffs the base in mock interest; it is the same tree he has already thoroughly frisked. He canters smugly back to the bench and we have a good laugh together. I will see that the old faker has a memorable supper tonight and, knowing that he will approve this plan, we will come back tomorrow with a package of peanuts for his friend.

The early-morning drunk, who has seen and heard none of this, drains his bag and tosses it onto the bare earth behind him. Time slows again as he forces himself to stand up. He sighs loudly, lashes out at the pigeon and shuffles off, the bird following close behind.

High in the sycamore tree Blackie sways back and forth, back and forth.

83

THE EXHIBITIONISTS

A group of artists and craftsmen are gathered on the sidewalk at the south end of the park under bright red and yellow and blue umbrellas, like a row of giant flowers. In the sultry November warmth it is difficult to escape the feeling that nature is playing tricks, that it is already spring. Even the pigeons are taken in, their sad courting rituals adding to the air of virtual unreality.

A ray of sunshine breaks through the slate-gray overcast and the drizzle ends immediately, as if someone has turned off a cosmic sprinkler. The huddled artists hurry to unveil their scattered canvasses, whose green lawns and shady trees contribute to the illusion that the world has turned upside down and the wrong season is upon us. Twice fooled, the pigeons redouble their efforts, the males puffing themselves up like feathery balloons to demonstrate their handsome colors and incipient virility. The females, playing hard to get, pretend to ignore them.

The artists, also puffed up, sit or stand amidst their chromatic wares, waiting for timid buyers to respond to their visual overtures. The wary shoppers, resisting the practiced attempts at seduction, gaze coyly at the proffered displays until, without warning, they approach one or another of the hucksters and a deal is quickly consummated.

The artists and pigeons aren't the only ones vying for attention. The park is full of people whose fashionable clothes, loud voices, tinted hair, heavy makeup, cellular phones, wild gestures, or swaggering demeanor shout, "Look at me!" Hardly anyone does, however; everyone is preoccupied with his own personal display.

In the midst of all this color and intensity a lonely old man with a thin, pointed face and dressed only in a raincoat abruptly opens it wide to demonstrate his own failed virility to a well-dressed woman, who gasps loudly, as if she has never seen the male organ. The pathetic creature struts around the park, repeating the overture to prospects of various ages and dispositions, eliciting everything from horrified cries to hearty laughter.

The police finally come to take away the grizzled Casanova, who has caused no real harm. Isn't it sad, Ben? He was just doing the same as everyone else, but all he had to show, after a lifetime of pain and sorrow, was himself.

84
The Preacher

All afternoon he follows us, quoting long passages from the Bible. Ben, who likes everyone, nonetheless keeps a dubious eye on the freelance evangelist, the other on me.

We have seen him before, this little man in his worn black suit, haranguing one or another passerby, following people out of the park to pursue them on their harried destinations. Always it is one-on-one, a personal salvation. Today it is our turn to face the self-appointed ambassador of God.

When I try to look into his sunken eyes I become terrified: they are those of death itself. Ben, who has no fear of dying, nonetheless senses my own discomfort and tugs at his rope.

His mouth is full of rotten teeth and his breath is bad. An excrescence protruding from the end of his nose does nothing to enhance his appeal. In a vain attempt to overcome my irrational apprehension I offer him a banana and two oatmeal raisin cookies, but he doesn't seem to notice. Nor does he pay the slightest attention to Ben, whose soul, evidently, is not worth saving. It is mine he is after, if it takes all day or, perhaps, eternity. Ben grabs one of the cookies but I have no appetite and stash the rest away.

Around and around the park we troupe, into and out of the restroom, on to the dog run, a quick stop at the Korean grocery, and still we cannot get away from the deep-set eyes and fetid breath. In desperation I lead Ben under the temporary scaffolding and up the front steps of the church across from the park; it is open and we barge in. Oddly, the wiry little preacher does not follow us here—perhaps he feels we have been safely corralled.

The sanctuary is deserted, and dark, too, except for the light coming through the stained glass windows. But it is quiet, though the air is a bit musty. Here in this familiar environment I sit down and try to collect my thoughts.

As I gaze at the silent organ I hear my mother singing beside me, unafraid, for an hour, of violent storms or metastasis. I was always puzzled by the power of this place, mystified by its message of unquestioning forgiveness. A terrible thought roars through my head: perhaps if I had learned this lesson better my father wouldn't have ended up the way he did....

C'mon, Ben—we can't hide here forever. I push open the heavy door and peer outside. It is a beautiful late afternoon; the park glows with fall color. The pretzel man pushes his cart along the street in front of the library, having finished today's chapter in his autobiographical saga. For the time being the man in black is gone.

85

Late Autumn

Only yesterday the plump trees were dressed in amber and ochre; today they are bare skeletons, all their finery stripped away by last night's wind and rain. The peace and beauty of autumn is only a sad and wonderful memory.

But no—not just yet! See the oak tree behind the statue of Garibaldi? About halfway up is a large, brick-red leaf—see it, Ben? As long as that leaf is there it will still be fall, never mind the chill in the air.

How quiet it is today; where is everyone—at autumn's funeral? Her demise, I feel, has been greatly exaggerated. Behold her ruddy leaf dancing gaily in the northwest wind. She endures! And look: the sun is coming out, and the pale brown earth has become a plain of solid gold!

But even the glorious sun appears to be cold—it pulls its blanket of cloud back over itself and the world is once again drab and bereft. The trees, vividly alive only yesterday, stand naked and shivering under the now-dismal sky. The few brave souls crossing the park hurry along briskly, their stiff brown collars turned up against the icy gusts.

Is it getting dark already? The trees quake at the prospect of night, yet autumn's brave leaf hangs on for dear life. The coming winter is a figment, a subject for tomorrow, and tomorrow will never come, not as long as— The leaf! Where is it? There it is! It's falling! Catch it! Catch it!

Oh my God—winter's here!

86

Change

A drunk leans close and whispers, perhaps prophetically: "If you're fuckin' hungry you can go down to the fuckin' seaport; the fuckin' people'll fuckin' feed you down there...." He offers me a snort, which I decline. He shrugs and moves off.

As I gaze sadly after him I absentmindedly open the door of the savings and loan. A fat woman clinks a coin into my cup. "Thank you, and have a nice day!" She pretends not to see or hear me.

Our mornings at the savings and loan are numbered. I have been told by well-meaning employees that the board of directors is considering a crackdown on the homeless who beg money from its patrons as they leave the institution. When they come to sweep us along I shall point out that we do not beg—we earn voluntary contributions by performing a service. If that fails we shall take our case to the courts, the guardians of our constitutional freedoms.

In the meantime I jingle our cup and accept whatever spare change our fellow man and woman elect to bestow upon us, though my heart is not in it, not with Otto and Mabel gone, the holidays approaching, and a pink slip in the offing.

They took Mabel away yesterday. She collapsed again and, after Ben found her, the rescue squad came to take her, half-consciously railing about the po-lice, to the emergency room. They left her postal cart where it was, in the corner of the park near the playground. Ben and I took it home with us so that no one would steal it, something that Otto always attended to before he, too, was taken in for repairs.

If you could see into the future, Ben, would you want to know how much longer we will be living in the park, sleeping under our sidewalk? Or, like me, would you prefer not to think about that?

"Thank you, and have a nice day!"

87

The Last Robin

A man dressed in a bathrobe and chewing on a teething ring crosses the park. At the corner a beggar falls to his knees to plead a coin from him. The man hands him the rubber donut and replaces it with an unopened box of toothpaste. Undeterred, the panhandler offers to sell him the teething ring. The man offers him the toothpaste for it. The farce continues until they disappear from sight.

Here come a group of students, laughing and yelling. They are happy: the holidays are approaching and they will be going home soon. Ben—there's a robin! But it is nearly Thanksgiving; shouldn't it have gone south by now? Is it lost, do you think, and doesn't know the way? Do you suppose it was separated from its parents in the heavy rain and strong winds we had last week and now it's homeless, like us?

But look: it's hurt. See how it tries to fly and keeps falling to the ground? There must be something wrong with its wing. Yet it keeps trying. Shouldn't we help it? If we could catch it we could take it to your doctor....

It's no use, my friend. Whenever we get close to it, it lurches away. Maybe we should leave it alone; perhaps we would only make the injury worse. We'd better let nature take care of it, as she has been doing for millions of years.

What are those kids up to? "Leave that bird alone!" What pleasure do they get torturing an animal, Ben, a creature that feels pain and anxiety just like us? Who is it that teaches cruelty to our children? Indifference and even hatred for anything different from themselves?

Where did it go—do you see it? There it is, half running, half flying into the bushes by the playground. See it there in the rhododendrons? How frightened it looks! And still the boys chase after it. "Hey! Leave it alone!"

Ben, who has never shown a splinter of anger, breaks free of my grip. Dragging his rope and barking loudly he charges at the young adolescents, who scatter like so many pins even before he can bowl them over. "You'd better watch that dog, mister!"

He trots back to me proudly, his head and his tail erect. "Good boy, Ben, good dog!"

The robin disappears into the bushes. It is safe for the moment; if those kids come back they won't be able to find it. But where will it stay when night comes? I'm afraid the rats will get it, Ben!

88

REPAIRS

Ben and I roll Mabel's bulky cart to the park this blustery morning, but she hasn't yet returned from wherever she is being treated. It is windy today, newspapers and other trash are blowing everywhere. But no matter, even on the best of days the city is strewn with garbage—the trucks can't keep up with it.

On the pockmarked street along the north edge of the park a repair crew has staked out a long-term claim, slowing traffic and filling the air with noise and dust. Most of the men look tired, even at the start of the day. They do their jobs well, but sluggishly, indifferently, as if their minds were on other, sweeter, things. One of them, clean-shaven and prematurely gray, looks up suddenly and I am momentarily shaken: it is the face of my father! But all their ruddy faces and hard hats remind me of him. Did I tell you that my old man was a construction worker, Ben?

On the opposite side of the park the big church is undergoing a facelift. The contrast between what has been cleaned and what has not is striking, the sandblasting having revealed breathtaking detail lost for years under tons of soot, a crude, if unintentional, metaphor for good and evil. Here, too, the workers proceed with diligence and skill, but with little enthusiasm.

In the park itself a crooked row of alabaster pipes awaits the reawakening of the lemon-yellow backhoe. Its driver has taken a break from digging up the clogged and broken water line, its ancient arteries having suffered a series of massive strokes months ago, slowing flow in the fountains and restrooms to a trickle. A long queue snakes out from the temporary facilities, a huge centipede in winter coats.

A trio of squad cars converge to a silent halt near the administration building. A dozens officers surround four diffident youths, frisk them roughly, if perfunctorily, and some of them haul the suspects away. The others proceed wearily to the next confrontation, another skirmish in the endless battle to halt the deterioration of the soul of man.

If we could fly, Ben, I suspect we would find what the pigeons already know: that the entire city is a catastrophe of broken facades, decaying infrastructures, ruined people, a gigantic beehive of repair crews performing a slow, neverending dance of renovation and renewal. Perhaps that is why all the workers look so tired, my friend; perhaps they realize the utter futility of their labors.

But wouldn't it be a glorious place if they ever got it finished—a city of free-flowing water, smooth streets, burnished buildings glowing in the sun, and honest, happy people?

89

Perspectives

In order to keep ourselves warm on this cold gray afternoon before Thanksgiving, Ben and I give ourselves a tour of the university, sunning ourselves in the light of the sciences and humanities. Perhaps because many of the students and faculty recognize Ben, no one takes much notice of us as we wander from building to building, though it seems more likely that we are simply invisible to eyes preoccupied with weighty academic matters. Even Jack the Ripper would very likely circulate unnoticed among these venerated halls.

When we come to the tall apartment building reserved for members of the faculty and their families I see that a new doorman has begun a lifetime of daily anxiety. Already he is beset by residents complaining about mail delivery, by a repair crew with no work order, by ringing telephones. On a sudden impulse Ben and I barge in and proceed smartly to the elevators. No one glances our way or speaks to us as we climb aboard and ride silently to the top floor, stopping twice to disgorge a passenger or two laden with ancient leather briefcases and newly-minted shopping bags.

The seventeenth floor is a rainbow of color, possibly to brighten the otherwise dull lives of its denizens. We do not tarry there, but proceed forthwith to the nearest stairwell and thence to the roof, where we step out into—the sky! From here we can see everything: to the west the river, a platinum gray strip under the low overcast, countless skyscrapers to the north and south, rows of apartment buildings to the east, and, directly below us, the park and its familiar surroundings. Look, there's Mabel, back from the hospital, dozing on her regular bench next to her beloved cart. But Ben cannot see over the retaining wall and, in any case, has his own agenda. I release him from his rope and he bounds away, stirring up a few birds on the far side. Even heaven has pigeons!

It is both awesome and humbling to be able to peer down on the world from a great height and, as Ben crunches around on the gravelly surface, I cannot tear myself away from the edge of the roof where I can observe secretly, from another dimension, the quivering life in the park below. There are the chess players, oblivious to the cold, and the pretzel man, accumulating incident and circumstance for his novel-in-progress. And the boys on their skateboards at the center of it all. How tiny, how vulnerable they appear from high above.

In the distance I catch the flashing lights of an emergency vehicle, which tries fruitlessly to thread its way through the afternoon congestion. Ben, who hears the far-off wail, whirls sadly behind me, his heart going out to the passenger struggling for breath inside. I think: how wonderful it would be to reach down and pluck up the little ambulance and drop it at the doors of the tiny hospital a mere inch or two to the east. And, as Ben rotates in frustration and impatience, I suddenly understand why a model barnyard or train depot is so fascinating to a child. For a little while he can fix all the world's problems. For a moment or two he can be God.

90

THANKSGIVING

I awaken on this pleasant Thanksgiving Day, my second on the streets and Ben's first, reminding myself that we have plenty to be thankful for. We have adequate food and shelter, something that much of the world does not. Except for the occasional cut or abrasion we enjoy good health. We have excellent neighbors, gainful employment, a place to relax and to play, and ample time to contemplate the beauty and tragedy of life. And we have our friends, especially Mabel, the pretzel man, and, of course, Crazy Otto, who has returned to the park after a two-week hiatus, a little more subdued, perhaps, but otherwise unchanged except for a close haircut. All that's missing are Allie and little Chris.

How I would love to call them, Ben, to hear their soft voices once more! Did I tell you I almost called Allie last Christmas? But what could I tell her? I did try to call Chris, but Grandma hung up on me! I shall never forget that evening, roaming the empty streets vacillating between rage and grief until the serenity of the cold, clear night, the bright, blinking lights, and the quietude brought a surprising and unexpected feeling of optimism and peace.

Someone shuffles by above our heads, stops, fiddles with the gate. Ben growls. The intruder quickly moves on.

I wonder what they are doing this very minute, don't you, my friend? Whether they are happy, whether they are thinking of me. Do you suppose Chris has forgotten what I look like? Would he recognize me, do you think, if I showed up at the door in my long hair and beard? How he would love to play a game of rubber newspaper with you! He would never forget to see that your water dish was full, as I sometimes do. And guess what—Allie has a back yard! With soft, green grass and a weeping willow tree, in whose shade you could rest after chasing the squirrels in the woods behind her house.

Have you ever known a beautiful princess, my friend, whose smile is as bright as the sun? Who is smart and funny and soft as a fresh, warm pretzel? Even this I have to be thankful for today—a wonderful year and a half with Allie, five with Chris. And, of course, all the happy months with you, who have shown me the beauty and serenity of the present, and given me the courage to face the future.

C'mon, Ben: let's go get the free breakfast the church has promised us!

91
FOG

Crazy Otto tells me the pigeon man is dead. They found him yesterday in his grubby apartment surrounded by fifteen dogs and twenty-six cats, who are homeless now, like us. He may have starved to death—he spent all his money on food for his pets, including the pigeons and squirrels in the park. Ben watches with interest as our comrade laughs heartily and lurches into the mist.

No, my friend, Otto has not disappeared, the world is simply obscured by fog, soft and quiet as the brown and white puppy who fell asleep in the dog run yesterday—do you remember? We are inside a cloud! Is it as wondrous and interesting as you expected it to be? Or does it seem unreal: people and dogs looming into existence and quickly fading out again, like those who come unexpectedly into our lives and then, just as abruptly, disappear?

Look, it's Brigitte! No . . . no, it's just someone who looks like her: young, beautiful, forlorn. See how she hurries to keep up with her mother, who frowns a step ahead of her? Too late—they've already disappeared.

Did I ever tell you how I got to know Allie? It was on a field trip and, yes, it was a foggy night. She came out of the mist and miraculously sat down in the seat on the train next to mine. We were both reading the same book—a French grammar—and by the time we got home the fog had lifted and we were already good friends. Now she is out there in all those clouds, maybe just a few feet away, for all I know. How I wish she would walk into my life again!

Listen: someone's humming. Oh, it's only Mabel singing one of her hymns, the still air magnifying and sweetening her prayer, like the song of a beautiful bird one cannot see. The surrounding silence adds to the illusion that we are alone in a great gray church, awaiting the end of time. The few people who scurry into and out of our solitary existence with their briefcases and anxious looks seem out of place here, and faintly ridiculous.

Mabel has stopped humming; it is so eerily quiet that we can pick up the pathetic cry of a man, perhaps miles away, mourning some unbearable loss. Ben's ears come up. He whines. The man is joined by a woman, sobbing. A little later, from a different direction, the scream of a child. Now I understand what Ben has been able to discern all along. In the fog I, too, can hear the terrible sound of hearts breaking.

92

CLEOPATRA

Sometimes, when we are working the door at the savings and loan, a tall, obviously wealthy woman comes in to reconsider her investments. She lives in a rent-controlled apartment nearby, Otto told me once, paying little more than Ben and I for housing. Although only in her early sixties, her leathery skin makes her look decades older. A cigarette dangles from her tiny, violent pink mouth, which appears to be drawn up by a tie string, like a bag of marbles. Her hands are long and thin and stuffed with a spaghetti of purple veins. In all the months we have opened the way for her she has never given us a penny.

Ben, who knows all the regular patrons by their step as well as their scent, comes awake to watch her throw the pink cigarette at our feet and clatter into the building. One eye glances up at me. I shrug. Unable to go back to sleep he rests his muzzle on his paws and gazes at the ankles of the fast-moving passersby.

Through the big window I can see Cleopatra waving her bankbook with one of her skeletal hands while the other pounds the desk of the astonished officer. Other customers look the other way and shuffle their feet uncomfortably. Someone yells at her to get in line. Undaunted, she continues the tirade.

For no explainable reason I come up with an outrageous idea. Ben, sensing my devilish glee, wags his tail. The man in the nearby magazine kiosk loans me a felt-tip marker and an inch of cellophane tape. From the corner trash can I filter out a relatively clean envelope. I return to Ben, who has remained at his post. In a moment my homemade bumper sticker is ready.

Cleopatra, still irate, her complaint not fully appreciated, stalks to the door and waits impatiently for me to open it. I pretend not to notice. Finally she bangs it ajar and rages out. One of Ben's eyes watches her closely. She hesitates momentarily, trying to remember whom she wants to harangue next. With all the delicacy of a summer breeze I fix the hand-lettered sign to the back of her fur coat. Sensing nothing, she lights another cigarette before striding furiously up the avenue, unaware that for the rest of the morning she will carry a little billboard advertising her offer to pay $100 to anyone willing to sleep with her. Unoriginal, and juvenile, too, but nonetheless gratifying.

Three of the regulars smile "good morning" as they depart the savings and loan, and each drops a dollar into my styrofoam cup. I can hear the man in the kiosk laughing. Later, he brings me two sugary doughnuts and a cup of coffee and pats Ben on the head. Everyone I see that day seems to be in a jovial mood, but maybe it is just my own.

93

The Fire Station

Often, when we pass by the fire station, we hear shouting and laughter emanating from the big open door where the trucks and equipment wait for disaster. Today it is quiet inside, and a black flag hangs from the top of the giant doorway. I surmise that a firefighter has been killed in the line of duty. But then I spot a photograph taped to the bright red bricks—it isn't one of the men who has died, but the Dalmatian whom we have seen on occasion hobbling on his arthritic hind quarters in front of the building.

SPARKY
our friend and companion
R.I.P, old buddy

As I read the epitaph one of the firemen comes out. He is thirty-something and stocky, with rust-colored hair, and clean-shaven except for a pair of extra-long sideburns. He wants to know if he can pet my dog. Without waiting for a response Ben flattens his whole body against the man's legs, nearly bowling him over. "Red"—including the quotation marks, according to the blue threads embroidered into his pocket—chuckles; it is the simple, uncomplicated laughter of a child. He grasps Ben's massive head in his hands and scratches his jowls briskly. Ben's eyes close in ecstasy.

"Red" motions us inside. We follow him to the big, shiny truck parked at the rear of the building, where he indicates we should wait. From here we can see a few other firefighters grouped around a table. A lively discussion, at whose center we seem to be, ensues. The fire truck is one of those long ones with a second steering wheel at the back. Suddenly I remember where we have seen Ben's new friend: he was the one driving the rear end of this very truck in the Memorial Day parade!

The conference abruptly terminates and "Red" returns to us. Taking a bandanna from his pocket he polishes an imaginary spot on the door of his dreams. "We'd like to buy your dog," he mumbles, without looking up. "Some of us have seen him around here, and we'd like to buy him."

Instinctively I head for the big door. This is the second offer I've had to "sell" my only friend and companion. How can you sell the moon and stars? Ben, to my annoyance, lags behind.

"You don't have to decide now," he calls after us. An afterthought, ending in a choke: "If you want to sell him, bring him in. We'll treat him good . . . ."

I hustle Ben to the street; he keeps looking back. Not, I think, because he wants to live at the fire station, though he probably would be happy there, but because he can sense the profound despair of a man who has lost an old and dear friend.

94

Cold Weather

We're freezing. The air is a frozen ether, so clear that we can almost see the stars. Ben's breath comes in short, smoky puffs, and he has grown a hoary mustache and a beard of tiny icicles. His left rear foot is bleeding, whether from the cold or cut by a shard of glass or ice I cannot tell.

For half the night we walk the streets, Ben wrapped in a large black plastic bag tied shut with a red ribbon found blowing in the park—a mobile, if lame, Christmas present. Unlike the evening last summer when we plodded this same route trying to find a cool place, the sidewalks are deserted. The fountain we splashed around in on that hellish night is frozen solid now, as if time were still, and the grass would feel like little brown knives under our feet. The campus buildings are all locked this time of night and, even if they weren't, the guards inside would motion us to move on. The lights on the Christmas trees inside the warm, silent apartments seem to glare at us mockingly.

The city shelter is too far away and, according to Otto, is unsafe. Numb with cold, we head for the nearest subway station, where we can at least get out of the wind.

Packed with others like us it is warmed by their bodies, if reeking of wine and urine. Ben sniffs out the last unoccupied spot, right beneath the ticket window, and is asleep immediately. I search his paw for sharp objects, finding only a clean cut, which has stopped bleeding already, and settle in against the booth. Though I cannot sleep it feels wonderful to sit down, to have warm ears and feet. In a few hours the cops will come to tell us we can't stay here and to clear the way for the city's employed. But that is a long time from now, an eternity, and, in the meantime, I can rest a little and imagine the smell of fresh, hot coffee. I see that I need a new pair of shoes.

Someone blows his nose on a tattered glove. I think I have never been so tired.

95

GOODWILL

Ben and I trek to the Goodwill store, hoping to find something we can afford. But the only shoes that fit me are going for four dollars, so we settle for a sound two-dollar comforter, though its purchase exhausts our life savings.

I peer out the front window and find Ben sitting in the warm sunshine. Ignoring the occasional pat of a friendly passerby, he focuses all his attention on the door. Certain that he is safe, I take a rare opportunity to browse, not to shop for goods but to poke shamelessly into other people's lives.

On an otherwise empty shelf sits a soft Teddy bear in excellent condition, if a little worn around the neck, a well-fingered puzzle titled "The Old Mill," and a set of enameled salt and pepper shakers shaped like a pair of howling coyotes, whose colors have faded somewhat, but which are still quite intact and eminently utilitarian.

Whose best friend was this bear? How many hands lovingly re-created this pastoral scene from a time gone by? How many eggs and soups were seasoned from the heads of the cream and mauve coyotes? Where are they now, those lost souls who have moved on to another, perhaps distant, life, or to an untimely grave?

When Mom died, and Dad closed the door on reality, I had to go through all her things, decide what to keep and what to discard, who might want this memento, that keepsake. She didn't leave much: half a closet of print dresses; a pair of tiny bronze shoes; a few porcelain birds; a turquoise glass dish won at the country fair; a green plastic statue of Abraham Lincoln, a souvenir of our trip to the nation's capital; old photographs of long-dead relatives; all my grade school tests and papers; a handprint etched in clay; a dented ashtray uncertainly smithed in shop class with a ball hammer, whose thin, smooth, brown handle I can still feel in my palm. Everything but the pictures, and my own personal history, went to Goodwill.

I scan the store for women's apparel, which is sequestered in tightly-packed racks near the back of the store. While Ben waits impatiently outside I make my way to that department, passing, along the way, the remains of other musty lives lived in quiet contentment or secret desperation—hats, books, records, typewriters, furniture. Finally I stand humbly before the dresses with their pink and blue flowers, in whose feel and smell I find my mother: young, smiling, and beautiful.

96

A New Life

It is never absolutely dark anywhere in the city, but the quietest time, if not the darkest, comes just before daybreak. I often lie awake listening to the scurrying of the rats and Ben's snoring, waiting for the pregnant night to deliver the dawn. But on this black morning he is wide-awake too: perhaps he hears something coming.

I dreamed I called Allie; a man answered. His voice sounded familiar, but I didn't recognize it. He went to find her, but before she could get to the phone we were disconnected. Do you know why I haven't called her for so long, Ben? Not because I have nothing to offer her, as I have implied. The truth is, I'm afraid to find that she no longer remembers or cares. Ben? Are you still awake?

It is cold again tonight—not so frigid as the night we spent in the subway station, but cold enough that Ben, though wrapped in the comforter and curled up against my body, shivers softly. Would you like to go live at the fire station, my friend? You would be warm there and I suspect you would get plenty of treats. Not just cookies and pretzels but real doggy goodies from colorful boxes like the kind you may have seen in the Korean grocery from your vantage point by the door. You would become fat, like Pfeiffer the Pekingese, of whom you are so fond!

Have you ever considered what would happen if we were evicted from our apartment here under the sidewalk? I could not keep you safe and warm if we had to sleep in doorways or on the street. And what if I got sick and had to go to the hospital? Who would feed you and take care of you then? There are at least a dozen good reasons why you would be better off in a good home, and I can think of no better place than the fire station, can you, my friend?

You liked "Red," didn't you? I know he would be a great pal to you. And think of this: your fondest wish would come true. You would not have to whirl in frustration whenever a fire truck sped by; you would be right there, doing your part to help those in distress. Your life would have meaning and purpose. Would they call you "Sparky," do you suppose?

Ben, who invariably gets right to the heart of the matter, whines and buries his head under my blanket.

I pat the lump under my hand. Never mind, my friend—if we die, we shall die together.

97

HELL'S ANGELS

The park is deserted except for Mabel, who hasn't yet gone to wherever she spends her nights. Because of the snow, which is still falling, the guards are late putting up the barricades, and we have stayed to absorb the silence and general serenity.

The pigeons have disappeared for the duration of the squall and, high in the oak trees, the squirrels sleep soundly in their nests. On the streets there is little traffic and no horns blare. The city is clean and dressed all in white tonight, an old tart playing the virgin.

But nothing lasts forever, and the perfect peace is shattered by the roar of half a dozen motorcycles, which slip and slide around the corner and blast into the park. Ignoring us, and indifferent to the possible response of the authorities, the bikers cross and re-cross the snowy terrain, the chrome studs on their black leather jackets flashing like stars in the intense light of the mercury lamps. Ben watches all this with keen interest: motorcycles have never intimidated him. But for his restraining rope he would already be romping with these big, loud beasts.

When the action has run its course the cyclists gather in the center of the park for a gab and a smoke, and it is still again.

The quietude doesn't last long. When they have finished their break they climb back onto their bikes and prepare to wreak havoc elsewhere. But one of the pack suddenly leaps off again, followed by the others. Simultaneously, like so many pigeons, they flop down in the snow. For some reason I am greatly moved by this puerile exercise, and I let go of Ben's rope. He bounds over to the group and they roughhouse with him for a while, running and chasing.

"Hallelujah!" Mabel sings. "Praise the Lo'd."

"Amen, sister!" shout the cyclists. Ben lopes back to me. As they remount, they wave a silent good-bye. One by one they kick their engines to a start and slowly, slowly, they roll to the street, roaring like a pride of lions.

Ben tugs me over to the big circle at the center of the park, where we find, in the powdery snow, deep impressions of eight perfect angels clad in studded leather jackets.

98

THE GOOD SAMARITAN

I wake up dizzy and weak, but I do what I must: I contribute to the portable urinal, feed Ben, and prepare to truck to the dog run and the savings and loan.

At the top of the steps I have to sit down, unable to go further. Ben empties his own bladder at the curb and licks my feverish face. As soon as I am able I scoot back down and crawl into bed, which is still made up, except for the paper-flat air mattress.

After more than a year on the streets without a sneeze I am ill. I doze off, or try to. There is nothing else I can do. Ben lies beside me, his massive head resting on my hip, his eyes, one at a time, surveying my own for nuance of expression, indication of change. Lying in that fitful state, halfway between wakefulness and sleep, I hear, or dream, the sound of a gate opening, footfall on the steps. "Hello?" A man cautiously appears. He is dressed in rags and wrecked shoes—he too is undoubtedly homeless, though his hair is cropped short and he is clean-shaven. Curiously, Ben does not snarl or bark, doesn't even raise his head. He whaps his tail softly against my leg. The man pats him, smiles at me. I feebly return it.

Neither of us speaks as he surveys the situation. "Be right back," he murmurs abruptly before disappearing up the steps, leaving me to wonder how he found us and the nature of his motives. But I am too sick to worry about it.

I doze helplessly, dreaming not of my family, of the glorious past or the uncertain future, but of Pavarotti, who strolls by singing a beautiful aria, to the cheers and applause of the entire neighborhood....

An hour—or maybe a week—later, the stranger reappears. This time he has brought something: a large paper cup of hot soup, a baguette of bread. I wag my head—I cannot even sit up to take them. Gently he slides a ragged arm under my shoulders, lifts me and props me against our cracked cement wall. He uncaps the soup, pulls a utensil from his coat pocket, raises a spoonful to my lips. The soup tastes wonderful, and from the first sip I begin to feel better, stronger. Silently he feeds me every drop, alternating with small chunks of bread, one or two of which he dunks and offers to Ben. Then he finds the bag of dry dog food and gives him his lunch. *Before* digging in, Ben licks his face.

While I watch Ben eat, the man starts silently up the steps. "Wait!" I call out, in a voice that sounds unfamiliar and strange. But he is gone, and I know I shall not see him again. I tell myself it was all a dream, that somehow I got better on my own and managed to feed Ben. But I am at a loss to explain the empty soup cup at my feet, the unfamiliar footprints in the dusty snow.

99

CHRISTMAS EVE

On our first annual Christmas Eve walk around the neighborhood Ben receives two beautiful gifts: a tremendous hug from a little boy and a tête-à-tête with a snow-white poodle called Fifi, who is almost lost inside a large red sweater. Her companion, a girl of about twelve, and I discuss weighty matters of names and ages while the dogs exchange holiday nuzzles, after which Ben and I continue our quest for colorful decorations and good cheer.

The Christmas tree lot reminds me of—everything. I try to pass it quickly, but Ben lingers to sniff the piney scent. The salesman, in the spirit of the season, offers us a wreath, at half price, which we can't afford. He ties a free sprig around Ben's neck; a canine Father Christmas, he marches off with an air of high expectation.

We stop in front of a large window filled with the reflective orbs and blinking lights of an aluminum spruce. On either side of the silvery tree, walls of books recede into the darkness, except for an expanse of brick suggesting a working fireplace. Stepping onto the lower railing of the iron fence I lift onto my toes hoping to share a bit of its glowing warmth. Although I can't quite see the fire, I imagine myself sitting in front of it on a comfortable sofa, my arm around Allie's soft shoulders, glass mugs full of nog on the flickering coffee table. But the drapes quickly swish shut, as if programmed to respond to inquisitive eyes.

We have better luck at the tiny French restaurant down the street, where a young man, noticing Ben and me peering into the darkened dining room—there is a fireplace here too, but it is unlit—leaves his smiling girlfriend at the table by the window long enough to bring us a couple of warm rolls before dashing back inside. Ben's is gone in a gulp, and he wags his tail at the smiling couple as I chew on my own. Through some incomprehensible magic I find myself sitting inside the cozy restaurant sipping red wine and gazing out at a young man in a ragged coat, who wishes he were in my place. The pretty girl I am with is my wife, the wife of our first Christmas together, whom I love very much, whose hand I squeeze—

A policeman barks: "Move along, buddy," and the bubble collapses. I wave and the couple inside wave back. Ben and I make our way down the street. The cop calls out, "Merry Christmas, friend!" I turn, but he is already around the corner.

A moment later we nearly bump into an elderly couple, who freeze for a second and then continue on their way, clinging to each other for dear life. The magic wand waves again and I see myself trying to help my aging wife out of the way of a homeless man and his dog. It is our last Christmas together.

I sit down on the curb and begin to sob. Ben licks my face, lapping up the tears, and I hug him as hard as did the little boy. I jump up and pound all my pockets for change. Two dimes and a penny. Then I remember: a collect call is free to the caller. Ben and I run to the public telephone on the corner, whose territory he adds to all his previous claims.

The recorded operator informs me that the entire trunk is busy, and politely suggests I place my call at a later time. Just as well, Ben—she wouldn't appreciate a call from me tonight anyway. Nonetheless, I hang up and immediately dial again: the line is now free. On the fourth ring Allie answers. She sounds distraught, sleepy. But she quickly accepts the call.

I immediately try to explain why I have tried to reach her late on Christmas Eve, but the words don't come out as easily as I had hoped. The fact is, I just wanted to hear her voice.

But it is she who does the fast talking. My father is going to AA meetings: he hasn't had a drink in months! He is back with Chris, who is still saving last year's present for me! They both want me to come home. She does, too....

I hear myself saying, "I'll be home for Christmas. Tell Dad and Chris I'll be home tomorrow." I don't mention Ben. He is my present to them.

"I love you," is the last thing I hear, and all I ever wanted to hear.

I wake up my wonderful orange friend and we hurry over to the church across from the park. It is almost midnight. The bells are chiming. Even for a would-be atheist like me the sound is rich with hope, warm with memory. A young man comes out of the church and invites me inside. I shake my head and motion toward Ben. "It's Christmas," he says. "Bring him in with you." I wipe off Ben's feet and we take a seat in the back pew. There aren't many people, but there is an abundance of candles, aglow with the beginning of time.

The organ begins to play. My spirits soar like the pigeons in the park across the street.

100

CHRISTMAS

It is after midnight when the Christmas Eve service is over. Ben and I amble across the park where we have spent most of our free time the past year. It is dull and brown now, but we recall its spring greens, its autumn golds, its summer rains and winter patinas of snow. It is resting at the moment, but we shall always remember it as a place of jugglers and musicians and jabbering youth, a carnival of color and excitement. Nor shall we forget Otto and Mabel and Vincent and the pretzel man and all the others who, except for the darkest hours, call this place their home. Nor Cleopatra, the old witch. May you live forever, Cleo!

A pair of pigeons cross our path, one white with black trim, the other its photographic negative. It has been said that when mankind destroys itself there will be nothing left but the insects. I say it will be pigeons. Long may they live! And the mice and rats and roaches and the squirrels, too, sleeping up there in the oak trees. Farewell, Blackie!

It is Christmas morning now and the park is almost deserted, though the gates haven't been put up yet and no one is chasing us out. Perhaps the attendants are leaving it open this joyous night.

Here come a trio of students, arm in arm, belting out a carol so loudly that the tune is lost. Ben and I stop to listen as they stumble past. One of them winks at me, another gives Ben a quick pat on the head, and they continue their happy journey without losing a beat. We shall miss the students too, their enthusiasm and vitality. Perhaps some day Chris, or my own son, will come here to study English or philosophy, and we will sit on our favorite bench and chew pretzels and watch life go on and on.

At the great red oak tree we turn and say our final farewells, Ben leaving a drop or two of perfume so that he won't be forgotten by all his friends. I have left something of his in the dog run as well: his chewed-up rubber newspaper, a present for Ben's favorite pal. Merry Christmas, Fricka! Happy New Year, Daisy, Pfeiffer and Duke! Good-bye, Sung Tieng! Good-bye, "Red"! Maybe we shall meet again some day!

Our own street seems particularly cheerful tonight. One or two residents have taken the trouble to drape with tinsel and glitter the little elms growing out of their tiny earthen plots next to the sidewalk, and to string a few bulbs on the wrought-iron gates. The apartments themselves are dark, but filled, I am sure, with the bright lights of love and hope.

One final time I open our own little gate and wire it shut again. Ben leaps down the steps and quickly disappears behind the trash cans he knows so well. I hear him snuffling loudly in the dark. Suddenly he reappears, following his nose along the little sidewalk to the door of the deserted flat. I soon see for myself what all the commotion is about: someone has been here. They have taken the air mattress, our blankets, all my extra clothes, and even our few cans of beans and dog food. Ben is still snorting around at the door, and I finally realize what he has known all along—the inhabitants of the empty apartment are back, home for the holidays and the new year.

It is a clear, cold night. I whisper for him to come and join me under the sidewalk, and we lie down close together. But I cannot sleep; I am thinking about Allie and Chris and, yes, my dad, who we will be seeing—today, if we can get a ride!—for the first time in more than a year. Yet, I will miss this place, and I am certain that Ben will, too.

After a while he begins to shiver. I hug him closer and try to think where we might find some newspapers or cardboard to sleep under. Ben grunts loudly as I rise to my knees. On a hunch I pry open the tight lids of the trash cans, our columnar wall for many months. Inside are the finest Christmas presents either of us has ever received: all our missing stuff is there, including my books, sketch pad, office supplies, the poem called "Ben"—the permanent residents have merely cleaned up their front yard!

In a few minutes our bed is made up, and Ben flops down again with a huge sigh. But he is still alert enough to accept a treat, which disappears with barely a crunch. "Merry Christmas, my friend," I say to him. He has no present for me, except the greatest gift of all: himself. He licks my face all over and, in another minute, is snoring. I lie down with my hands behind my head, looking up at the stars which I cannot see but which I know are there.

visit the author at www.genebrewer.com

CPSIA information can be obtained
at www.ICGtesting.com
Printed in the USA
BVHW030710100219
539881BV00004B/13/P

9 781425 718794